Cassie the Cat

Pedro the Penguin

Chesney the Cheetah

Zoe the Zebra

Sonia the Snow Rabbit

Paul the Python

First published in hardback in 2012 by Hodder Children's Books
This edition published in 2012

WWW.GETWELLFRIENDS.COM

Hodder Children's Books, 338 Euston Road, London, NW1 3BH
Hodder Children's Books Australia, Level 17/207 Kent Street, Sydney, NSW 2000

A catalogue record of this book is available from the British Library.

ISBN: 9781 444 90069 9

Hodder Children's Books is a division of Hachette Children's Books
An Hachette UK Company
www.hachette.co.uk

CHESNEY
runs into Trouble!

Kes Gray & Mary McQuillan

A division of Hachette Children's Books

Hello! I'm Nurse Nibbles,

and these are my **get well friends.**

In my home, I have lots of hospital beds of ALL shapes and sizes.

Which is a good job because poorly animals come to visit me from ALL over the world!

I've looked after ferrets with fractures,

tigers with toothache,

jellyfish with jaundice,

snails with sniffles,

and even llamas with laryngitis.

This morning a new poorly patient came to see me. His name was Chesney the cheetah and he looked very odd indeed.

This is the story of how Chesney the cheetah ran into trouble...

One day, Michael the meerkat was training Chesney the cheetah for the Champion of Champions Cheetah Championship Chase Race.

"Let me climb on your back, Chesney," said Michael. "If you can learn to run fast with a meerkat on your back, you'll be able to run even faster when I'm not there."

And Michael was right!

The next day, Michael arrived with a zebra.

"If you can learn to run fast with the two of us on your back, Chesney, you'll be able to run super fast when we're not there."

And Michael was right.

The following day,
Michael turned up
with the zebra and
a rhino!

"Chesney, if you can learn to run fast with all three of us on your back, you'll be able to run super-duper fast when we're not there."

And Michael was right again.

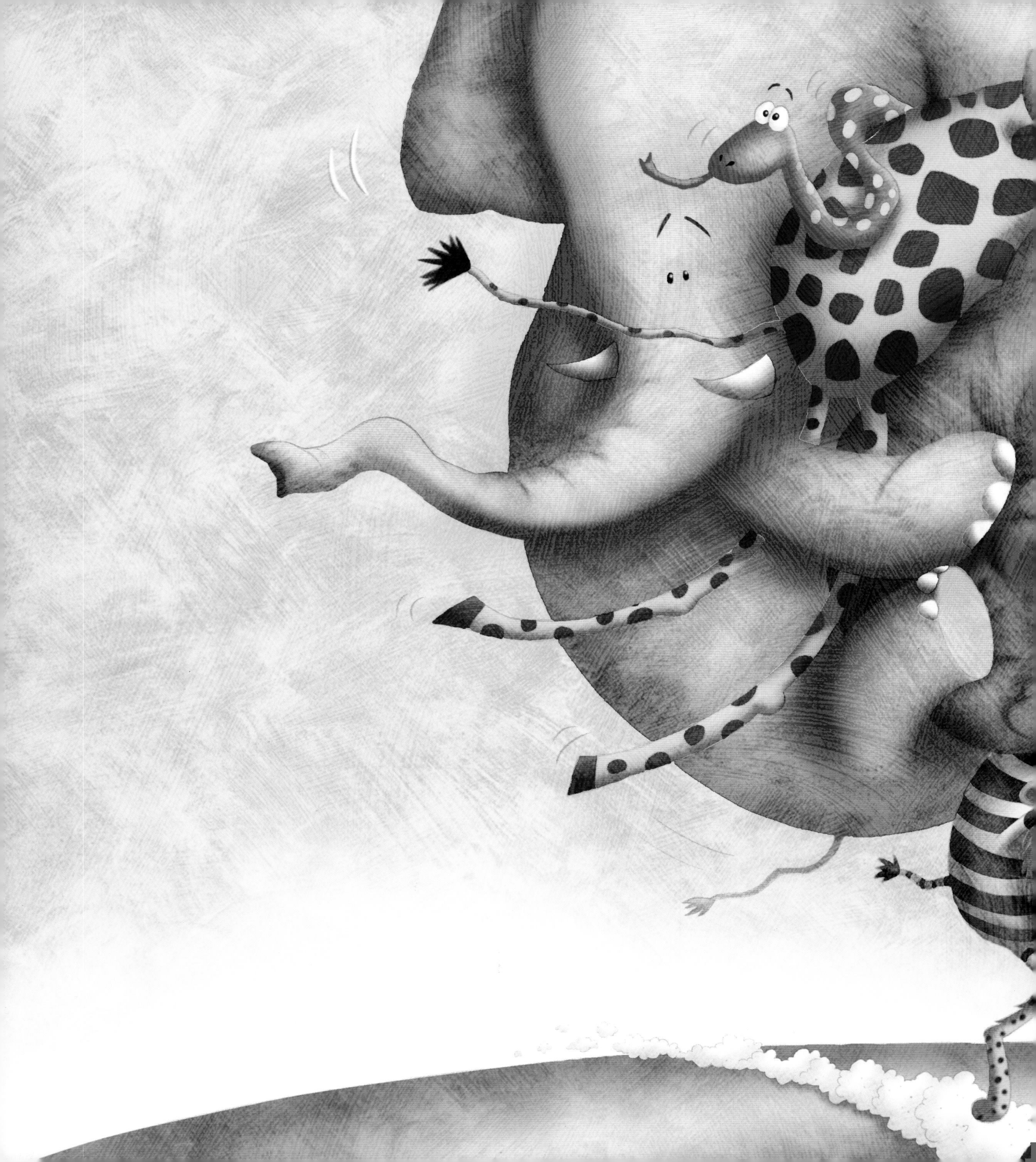

Every day, Michael trained Chesney
as well as he possibly could.

By the start of the race, Chesney was fitter and faster than he had ever been in his life.

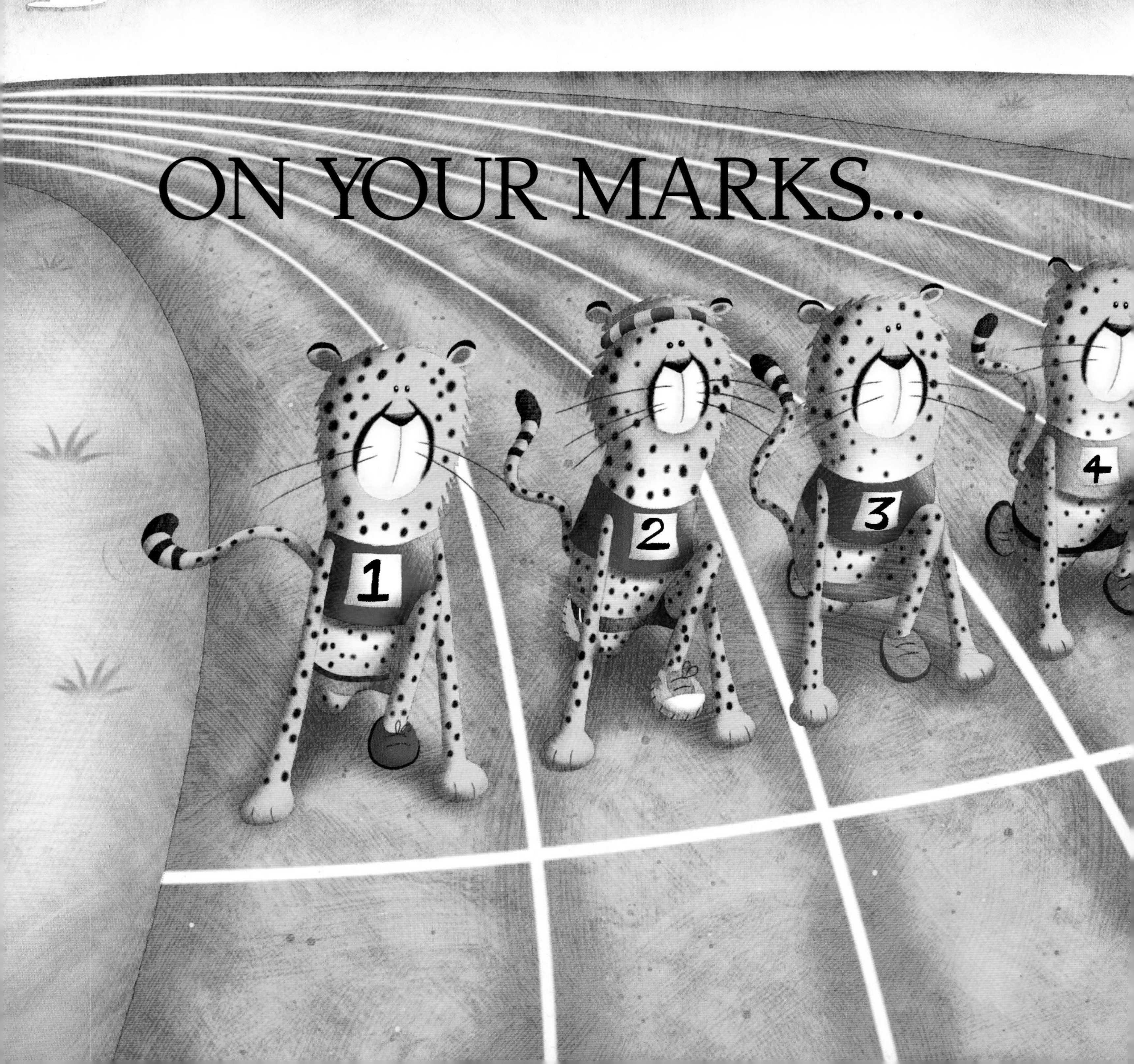

GET SET...

By the 'G' of 'GO!', Chesney was halfway down the track!

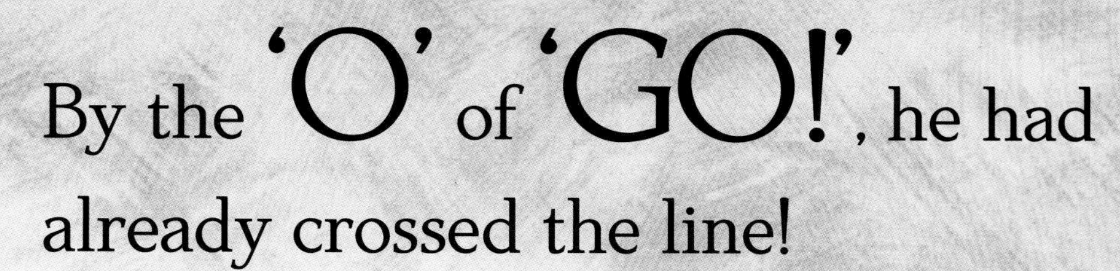

By the 'O' of 'GO!', he had already crossed the line!

Chesney raised his paws
triumphantly as his
chest broke the ribbon.

He had won the Champion of Champions Cheetah Championship Chase Race in a super-duper-wuper fast time!

But there was one problem. His spots had fallen off along the way!

"Oh, dear!" said Michael. "You ran so fast, Chesney, your spots couldn't keep up!"

Oh dear indeed!

No wonder Chesney came to see me.

Never mind. The good news is that Chesney won first prize for taking his medicine, and was champion at putting his feet up too.

He began to feel better in record time, and I'm pleased to report that Chesney the super-fast cheetah did get his spots back in...

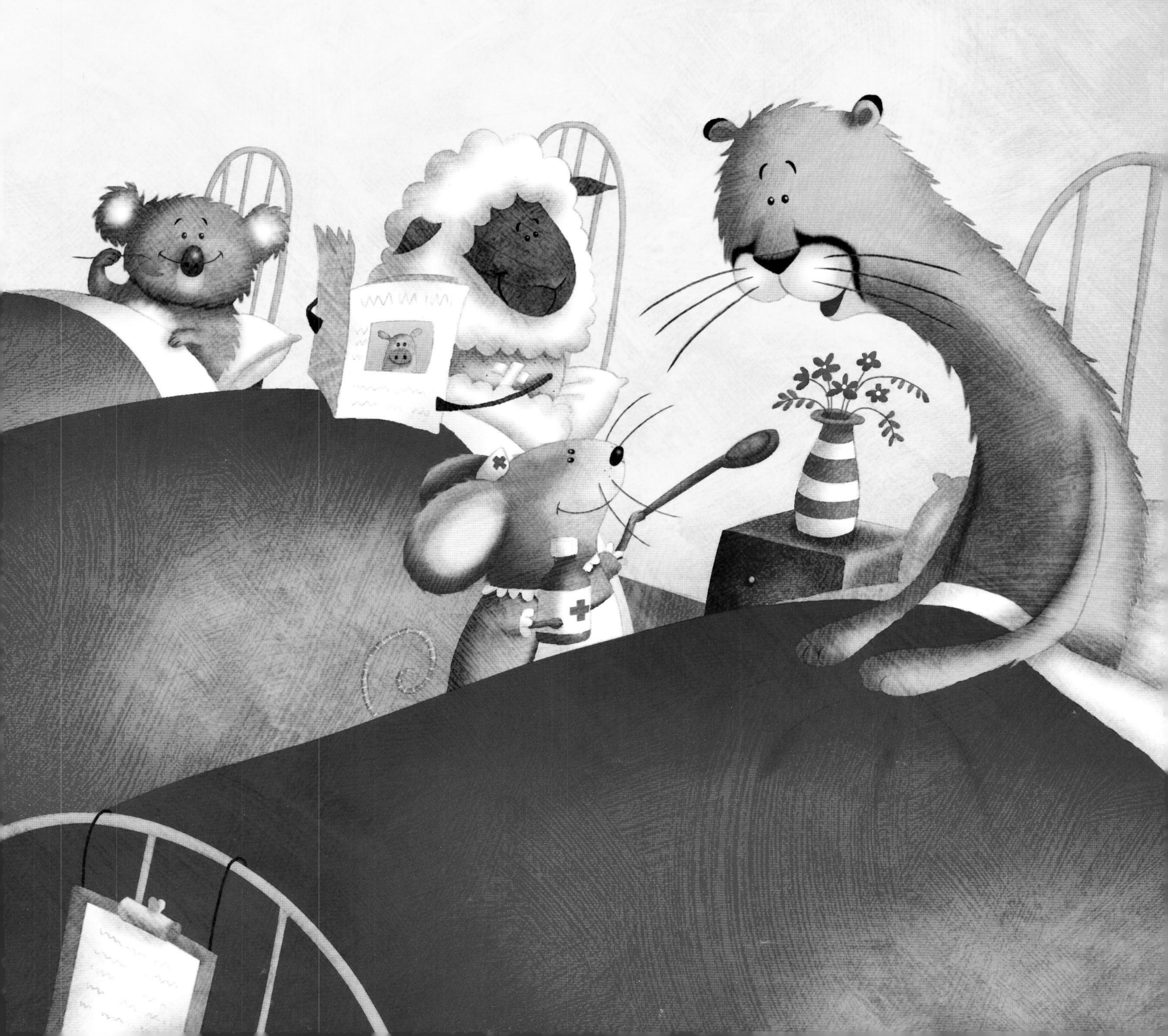

... THE END!

Emo the Elephant

Beyonce the Bear

Nurse Nibbles

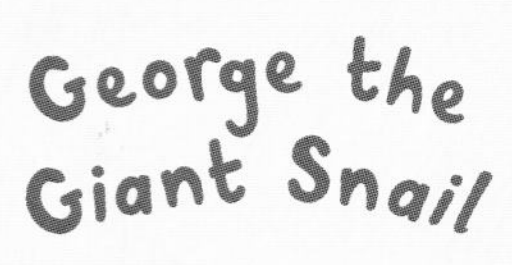

George the Giant Snail

Momo the Monkey

Giselle the Giraffe

Cassie the Cat

Pedro the Penguin

Zoe the Zebra

Chesney the Cheetah

Sonia the Snow Rabbit

Paul the Python

NURSE NIBBLES SAYS:

Show **CHESNEY** how much you care by giving him a sticker.

Emo the Elephant

Beyonce the Bear

Nurse Nibbles

Momo the Monkey

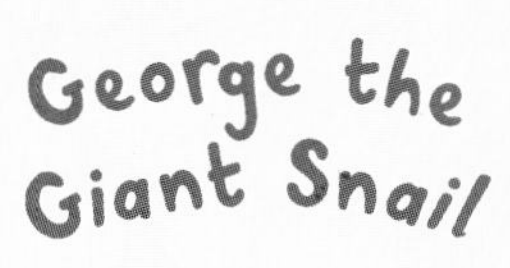

George the Giant Snail

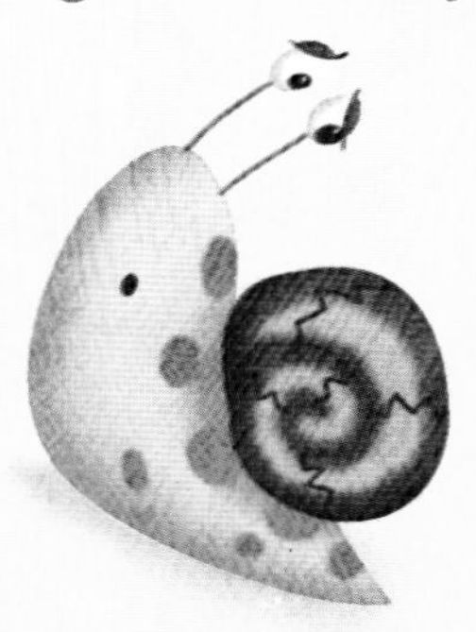

Giselle the Giraffe

Did you know?

FASCINATING FACTS FROM
ENCYCLOPAEDIA BRITANNICA

Illustrated by Paul Hogarth

ENCYCLOPAEDIA BRITANNICA INTERNATIONAL, LTD.
LONDON

Encyclopaedia Britannica first began to appear in weekly sixpenny numbers in December 1768, in Edinburgh. Early in the 19th century it established the tradition of obtaining contributions from the great authorities of the day. By the time the present 15th edition appeared, it had more than 4,000 contributors, from all over the world. Their major articles are grouped in the 17 volumes called the Macropaedia. Shorter articles for ready reference are found in the 12 volumes called the Micropaedia.

International Standard Book Number 0-85229-201-5

Typeset by CCC, printed and bound in Great Britain by
William Clowes Limited, Beccles and London

The story of Abraham: folklore or history?

There can be no biography of Abraham in the ordinary sense. The most that can be done is to apply the interpretations of modern historical finds to biblical materials so as to arrive at a probable judgment as to the background and the events of his life. This involves a reconstruction of the age of Abraham, Isaac, Jacob, and Joseph which until the end of the last century was unknown and considered virtually unknowable. It had been assumed that the narratives concerning the patriarchs were only the projection of the situation and concerns of a much later society, and of little historical value.

Archaeologists have since discovered many monuments and documents that date back to the age of the patriarchs in the traditional account. The excavation of the royal palace at Mari, an ancient city on the Euphrates, for example, brought to light thousands of cuneiform tablets which help show that, in the biblical book of Genesis, narratives fit perfectly with what is known today of the early 2nd millennium BC from other sources, but imperfectly with a later period. This result has aptly been termed "the rediscovery of the Old Testament."

See ABRAHAM in volume 1 of the Micropaedia.

What is adobe?

Adobe is a Spanish word for sun-dried clay bricks, or a structure built from such bricks, or the clay soil from which the bricks are made.

The usual method of making adobe bricks is to wet a quantity of suitable soil and allow it to stand for a day or more to soften and break up clods. A small quantity of straw or other fibrous material is added, and the materials are mixed with a hoe or similar implement. The mass is then trampled with bare feet. The adobe is shaped into bricks in four sided molds, open at top and bottom. The bricks are allowed to dry partially while flat on the ground; they are then stacked on edge to permit more thorough and uniform drying.

Adobe walls are normally built on a solid, waterproof foundation. The bricks are laid in a mortar of the same material, then finished with a coat of adobe, or with lime or cement plaster. With proper construction and maintenance, an adobe wall may last centuries. Adobe has remarkable insulation properties.

See ADOBE in volume 1 of the Micropaedia.

What African city controlled the Mediterranean?

The western part of North Africa, comprising modern Morocco, Algeria, and Tunisia, forms a well-marked zone completely surrounded by sea or desert. This is Maghrib, or Barbary. The earliest settlements here from outside were those of the Phoenicians in Tunisia, where they founded Carthage. This city-state was built on a site with many natural advantages, at one of the few sheltered points of the Barbary coast. It commanded the passage between the eastern and western Mediterranean and so controlled the western Mediterranean for more than 600 years. The Carthaginians were interested primarily in maritime trade and made little attempt to penetrate far from the coast. Their activities were concentrated in a series of trading posts along the coasts of the Mediterranean and the Atlantic to where the desert again comes down to the sea. Isolated expeditions pushed on much further than this; Hanno in the 5th century BC voyaged at least as far as the area of modern Sierra Leone.

See AFRICA in volume 13 of the Macropaedia.

Where do the Ainu live?

In Hokkaido, Sakhalin, and the Kuril Islands live a people called the Ainu. They are physically quite unlike their Mongoloid neighbours, with the most profuse body hair of any known group. Ainu once lived on all four of the major Japanese islands, but were pushed northwards over the centuries. The Ainu language has been largely supplanted and there are hardly any pure Ainu left. Traditionally, the chief Ainu ritual involved the sacrifice of a bear.

See AINU in volume 1 of the Micropaedia.

Who gave his name to America?

Born in Florence in 1454, Amerigo Vespucci was a navigator and explorer of the New World contemporary with Columbus. In the service of first the Spanish and then the Portuguese government, Vespucci is believed to have discovered the mouth of the Amazon river. He thought the coast was that of the extreme easterly peninsula of Asia, but in the course of another voyage in 1501–2 he became convinced that the newly discovered lands were not part of Asia but a "New World". In 1507 Martin Waldseemüller printed a Latin version of Vespucci's travels, preceded by a pamphlet of his own in which he suggested that the newly discovered world be named "From Amerigo the discoverer . . . as if it were the land of Americus or America." The extension of the name to North America came later.

Some scholars have held that Vespucci was an ignorant usurper of the merits of others. The fact that Spain entrusted him, a foreigner, with the office of chief navigator is sufficient to dispose of these accusations. The Spaniards saw that he possessed an outstanding knowledge of nautical science, and that he was a man to whom confidential matters could be entrusted.

See VESPUCCI, AMERIGO in volume 12 of the Micropaedia.

What was the Amphibolos?

The American engineer Oliver Evans (1755–1819), after a long period of neglect, is now recognized as an important pioneer of the Industrial Revolution. He obtained the U.S. patent for the high pressure steam engine in 1790, and went on to work on it for several years, envisioning both a stationary engine for industrial purposes and an engine for land and water transport.

By placing both the cylinder and the crankshaft at the same end of the beam, instead of at opposite ends, Evans created an engine with potential for road transportation. He was however unable to persuade the authorities to permit its use on the Philadelphia Turnpike – not unnaturally, since it might well have frightened the horses. Within a few years he had engines doing other kinds of work, and in 1805 completed his steam-engine scow, called the Orukter Amphibolos or Amphibious Digger. Equipped with wheels, it ran on land as well as water, making it the first powered road vehicle to operate in the United States.

See EVANS, OLIVER in volume 4 of the Micropaedia.

How do animals find their way?

An animal finds its way home by remembering what it saw or smelled on the way out. This process is common to all creatures, including birds, insects, and fish. The eel, which travels great distances across the ocean, is believed to find the way back by remembering traces of smell in the ocean around. Birds, on the other hand, navigate almost entirely by sight and are extraordinarily adept at recognizing landmarks from the air.

When a young bird migrates, it instinctively aligns itself in a certain direction, flies until it has no more energy, and then lands. To set out in the right direction, the bird instinctively uses the Sun by day or, by night, reacts to the pattern of stars around the pole. To use the Sun by day, the bird has to make allowances for the change in direction from rising through to setting. It therefore needs a timing instinct that can correct for the passage of the Sun across the sky. Insects and fish, too, have such timing instincts.

See NAVIGATION in volume 24 of the Macropaedia.

How thick is the ice in Antarctica?

The continent of Antarctica is almost wholly overlain by a continental ice sheet, containing about 90 percent of the world's ice. The average thickness is about 2,000 metres. Around the Antarctic coast, shelves, glaciers, and ice sheets continually "calve", or discharge, icebergs into the seas.

Because of this vast ice, the continent supports only a primitive indigenous population of cold-adapted land plants and animals. The surrounding sea is as rich in life as the land is barren.

Antarctica was ice-free during most of its lengthy geologic history, and there is no reason to believe it will not become so again in the probably distant future. Effects of the melting ice will be world-wide, for sea level will rise possibly as much as 45 or 60 metres.

See ANTARCTICA in volume 13 of the Macropaedia.

What is anthropology?

Anthropology, the science of man, is concerned with the study of human differences and was born after the Age of Discovery had opened up societies that had remained outside the technological civilization of the modern West. In fact, the field of research was at first restricted to those societies that had been given one unsatisfactory label after another: "savage", "primitive", "prehistorical", and so on. What such societies had in common, above all, was being the most "different" or the most foreign to the anthropologist; and in the early phases of anthropology, the anthropologists were always European or North American.

Anthropologists today study more than just primitive societies. Their research extends not only to village communities within modern societies but also to cities, even to industrial enterprises. Small-scale societies are simpler or at least more homogeneous than modern societies and change at a slower pace, so are easier to see whole.

See SOCIAL SCIENCES in volume 27 of the Macropaedia.

When were antibiotics first used?

Attempts to use substances derived from one organism to inhibit or kill others began at least 2,500 years ago, when the Chinese became aware of the curative properties of moldy curd of soybeans and used this substance to treat boils, carbuncles, and similar infections. The first suggestion that bacterial antagonism might be important in treating disease was made by two Frenchmen, Louis Pasteur and Jules-François Joubert in 1877. They had discovered that the bacteria responsible for an infection called anthrax grew rapidly if inoculated into urine free from micro-organisms but died if so-called common-air bacteria were present.

The antibiotic era did not begin, however, until about 1928, with the discovery by Sir Alexander Fleming that a growth culture of the pus-producing bacterium, *Staphylococcus aureus*, had disappeared in an area in which a green mold was growing. Since the organism that produced the substance that killed the bacteria was a species of *Penicillium*, Fleming named the substance penicillin. Attempts to treat human infections with this material were not encouraging, however, because the substance was unstable and lacked potency. Not until several years later did several workers at Oxford University examine the possibility that stable penicillin might be produced in large enough quantities to treat human disease. In 1941 the drug was used to treat serious infections; the results were dramatic, as patients who received penicillin made rapid and complete recoveries. Since 1948, a large number of substances have been discovered which inhibit or kill bacteria and some fungi.

See DRUGS AND DRUG ACTION in volume 17 of the Macropaedia.

What do we owe to Nicolas Appert?

In commercial canning, carefully prepared raw food is placed in a sealed container, subjected to definite high temperatures for the proper period of time, and finally cooled. Heating the contents of the can destroys spoilage organisms that may be present, and reinfection through exposure to air is prevented by the can's permanent seal.

Nicolas Appert, a Parisian confectioner, first succeeded in preserving certain foods in glass bottles that had been kept in boiling water for varying lengths of time. In 1810 his work was published in a treatise entitled *L'art de conserver, pendant plusieurs années, toutes les substances animales et végétales*. Appert could give no logical explanations for the effects of canning, but believed that the application of heat to a sealed container, together with the exclusion of air, combine to retard or eliminate the process of decomposition. Bacteriology was unknown, and a half century passed before the true causes of food spoilage came to be understood.

Peter Durand, an Englishman, conceived the idea of using tin cans instead of bottles. By 1839, tin-coated steel containers were widely used.

The sanitary or open-top can, developed about 1905–08, eliminated the use of solder in sealing the can, and a perfect closure was guaranteed by the double seamed top and bottom.

See FOOD PROCESSING in volume 19 of the Macropaedia.

How does the archaeologist date his discoveries?

Many material remains of man's past have no dating problem: they may be, like coins, self-dating, or they may be dated by man-made dates in written records. But the great and difficult part of the archaeologist's work is dating material remains that are not themselves dated. This can be done in one of three ways.

Cross dating. Sometimes an object from another culture whose date is known (*e.g.* in the case of pottery, by its style) is found at a previously undated site. Or, an object from an undated culture may be found at a site whose date is known. This is known as cross dating. Much of the prehistoric chronology of Europe in the Neolithic, Bronze, and Early Iron ages is based on cross dating with the ancient Near East.

Relative dating. Stratigraphy is the essence of relative dating. In excavating, the archaeologist can establish the chronology of the different layers or strata of the earth in which the artifacts and human remains are found. There may, however, still be doubt as to whether all that is found in the same level is contemporary. The analysis of the fluorine content of bones has been very helpful here. If bones in apparently the same geological or archaeological level have markedly different fluorine content, then it is clear that there must be interference, for example, by a later burial, or by deliberate planting of faked remains, as happened in the case of the Piltdown "Man" hoax in England.

Radioactive carbon dating. The greatest revolution in prehistoric archaeology occurred in 1948, when Willard F. Libby, at the University of Chicago, developed the process of radioactive carbon dating. In this method, the activity of radioactive carbon (carbon-14) present in bones, wood, or ash found in archaeological sites is measured. Because the rate at which this activity decreases in time is known, the approximate age of the material can be determined by comparing it with carbon-14 activity in presently living matter. There have been problems and uncertainties about the application of this method, but it has given archaeology a new and absolute chronology that goes back 40,000 years.

See THE STUDY OF HISTORY in volume 20 of the Macropaedia.

Did Archimedes have a brainwave in the bath?

Far more details survive about the life of Archimedes than about any other ancient scientist, but they are largely anecdotal, reflecting the impression that his mechanical genius made upon the popular imagination. Thus, he is credited with inventing the Archimedes screw, a device for raising water, and he is supposed to have made two "spheres" that Marcellus took back to Rome – one a star globe and the other a device (the details of which are uncertain) for mechanically representing the motions of the Sun, Moon, and planets. The story that he determined the proportion of gold and silver in a wreath made for Hieron is probably true, but the version that has him leaping from the bath and running naked through the streets shouting "Heureka!" ("I have found it!") is popular embellishment. Equally apocryphal are the stories that he used a huge array of mirrors to burn the Roman ships besieging Syracuse; that he said, "Give me a place to stand and I will move the world", and that a Roman soldier killed him because he refused to leave his mathematical diagrams.

See ARCHIMEDES in volume 13 of the Macropaedia.

How does the architect use space to create feelings?

The painter suggests space, the sculptor fills it, the architect envelops it, creating a wholly human and finite environment within the infinite environment of nature. The concept that space can have a quality other than emptiness is difficult to grasp. When a building is entered, floor, supports, walls, and a ceiling are seen, all of which can be studied and perhaps enjoyed, while the space, in the sense that one is accustomed to think of it, is void: the absence of mass, filled by air.

But spatial experiences that express something are common to everyone, though they are not always consciously grasped. One feels insecure in a low cave, exhilarated and powerful on a hilltop. These are psychological and motor reactions that result from measuring one's potential for movement against the surrounding spaces. An infinite variety of such reactions may be summoned by the architect, because he controls the limits above, below, and on all sides of the observer. In the nave of a Gothic cathedral the high walls closely confining the observer on two sides restrict his possible movements, suggesting advance along the free space of the nave towards the altar; or their compression forces him to look upward. The experience of Gothic space is called uplifting because it urges one to rise.

See THE ART OF ARCHITECTURE in volume 13 of the Macropaedia.

Australopithecus: man or ape?

Australopithecus (literally "southern ape") was the generic name given to the first discovered member of a series of fossils of creatures closely related, if not ancestral, to modern human beings. Since the first discovery – of a child's skull in a cave at Taung, South Africa, in 1924 – similar hominid remains have been found at numerous sites in East and southern Africa.

The term australopithecine is often used to refer to all the fossil hominid material that dates between 8 million and 1½ million years ago, filling the gap between the fossil apes and *Homo erectus* ("upright man"). There are few hominid fossils from the period up to 3,500,000 years ago, but after that date the fossil record is much richer and open to varied interpretations. Some scholars have seen the fossil evidence of the australopithecines as merely representing various stages within a single evolving lineage leading to *Homo erectus*, while others have suggested that there may have been two, or even three, lineages evolving in parallel, only one of which led to the later species of *Homo*. Whichever is the case, the study of australopithecines is regarded as the study of one of the most important stages in the emergence of *Homo sapiens*.

See HUMAN EVOLUTION in volume 18 of the Macropaedia.

How much can a newborn baby sense?

A newborn human being is a remarkably capable organism. From the moment he begins to breathe, he normally behaves as if he can see, hear, smell, and is sensitive to touch, painful stimulation, and changes in position. Perhaps taste is not yet functioning during the first day after birth.

The newborn has a variety of reflexes, many of which are complex. An infant only two hours old typically will follow a moving light with his eyes, will show dilation and constriction of his pupils as darkness changes to light, will suck almost anything (*e.g.*, a finger) inserted into his mouth, and will turn his head in the same direction as the side on which his cheek or the corner of his mouth is touched.

The newborn baby can cry, turn away, vomit, lift his chin from a front position, and grasp an object placed in his palm.

See THE DEVELOPMENT OF HUMAN BEHAVIOUR in volume 14 of the Macropaedia.

Where do bacteria live?

Bacteria are single-celled micro-organisms, among the smallest living creatures known.

Bacteria are ubiquitous, occurring in virtually every conceivable environment: from polar ice to hot springs; from mountain tops to the ocean deeps; from plant and animal bodies to forest soils. Most are active in environments in which the temperature is above 5°C; some are exceptional in being active in temperatures near or slightly below 0°C. The upper limit is around 30°C for soil bacteria and 37°C for animal parasites; the maximum temperature, above which growth does not occur, is around 70°C. Some survive in a dormant (or spore) state, reviving when conditions become more favourable. This capability has allowed bacteria to become perhaps the most widespread organisms on Earth.

See BACTERIA in volume 14 of the Macropaedia.

How did Baedeker give tourists the freedom of Europe?

In 1829 Karl Baedeker brought out a guidebook to the town of Koblenz, but the system on which his famous series of guides was based was evolved in a guide to part of the Rhine. Baedeker's aim was to give the traveller the information necessary for him to dispense with paid guides. He checked the reliability of his books by making incognito journeys. A notable feature of the Baedeker guides was the use of "stars" to indicate objects and views of special interest, as well as to designate reliable hotels. By the time of his death much of Europe had been covered by his guidebooks.

See BAEDEKER in volume 1 of the Micropaedia.

What did the earliest ballet dancers wear?

In the earliest ballets of the 17th century, dancers traditionally wore heeled shoes. Men wore the costume *à la Romaine*, or *tonnelet*, a stiff, bellshaped wired skirt of brocade or similar material, resembling in shape the modern tutu. Women wore heavy costumes reminiscent of court dress with wigs, elaborate trains, and jewels. Male and sometimes female dancers wore leather masks, comic or tragic in appearance, that represented the character portrayed and concealed all facial expression.

In the early 18th century the ballerina Marie Camargo shortened her skirts to midcalf, invented heelless dance slippers, and wore close-fitting drawers to facilitate and exhibit her mastery of intricate dance steps.

See COSTUME, BALLET in volume 3 of the Micropaedia.

Who first flew in a balloon?

The most important pioneers in balloon development were the French brothers Joseph and Étienne Montgolfier. Watching smoke rise in the chimney, they concluded that it possessed some mysterious property, which they called "levity". They made up a small silk bag, which they held over a fire. It filled with smoke and, when released, rose to the ceiling. Later, the Montgolfiers invited all the citizens of their home town of Annonay to witness an ascension of their "Globe Aérostatique". This was a spherical bag about eleven metres in diameter made of light fabric backed by paper. Held over a smoky fire, it rapidly inflated, and is said to have drifted more than 2 kilometres from its starting point.

Hearing of the Montgolfiers' performance, the Parisian physicist J.-A.-C. Charles attempted to duplicate it, using the newly isolated gas hydrogen. The balloon of varnished silk was released from the Champ de Mars on August 27, 1783 and descended some 24 kilometres away. The local peasants, alarmed by the apparition descending from the clouds, attacked the "monster" with scythes and pitchforks and tore it to pieces.

On September 19, Joseph Montgolfier released a balloon from the Great Court at Versailles carrying a sheep, a rooster, and a duck. They survived the ordeal, and the stage was set for the first manned flight. At first it was proposed that a pair of condemned criminals be used for the experiment. One Jean-François Pilâtre de Rozier, who had volunteered for the flight, protested that such were not worthy of the honour of being first to take to the air. In this he was joined by François Laurent, marquis d'Arlandes, who wished to share the adventure. Louis XVI finally gave his consent, and on November 21, 1783, the two men took off in free flight from the Bois de Boulogne, Paris. They stayed in the air for 23 minutes, reached a height of 900 metres, and travelled 16 kilometres.

See TRANSPORTATION in volume 28 of the Macropaedia.

Why do bees dance?

A bee colony is a family community of which every individual is an integral unit. The life of the honeybee colony is potentially endless: the continued survival of the colony results from the fact that young queens replace the old. The degree of social organization in the colony is most evident in the division of labour. Tasks are assigned according to age. After performing tasks within the hive (such as cleaning, brood nursing, and comb building) a worker bee becomes, after about 20 days, an entrance guard, and finally a collector, remaining at this job until her death.

The highly integrated activities of the colony require sophisticated methods of passing information among its members. The dance of the honeybee is perhaps the most remarkable. After

a bee has discovered a new source of food, she tells other bees about it by means of various dancelike movements. If the food source is near the hive, a "round" dance is performed. A "tail-wagging" dance indicates that the food source is more than 80 metres away. An upward tail-wagging run means "The flight is towards the sun". The bees also dance when the swarm is searching for a new dwelling, in order to report the whereabouts of a suitable nesting place.

See INSECTS in volume 21 of the Macropaedia.

What is bioelectricity?

Electricity can be generated in animal tissue. It is a cellular phenomenon, enabling the nervous system to exhibit rapid response. Bioelectric phenomena are mainly fast signalling in nerves or triggering of physical processes in muscles or glands, and are found in all living organisms.

In a few animals, notably the electric fish, adaptations have occurred so that electric current generated in the body cells can be utilized. In some species the current is used for sensing purposes, while in others it is used to stun or kill prey. In such adaptations voltages from many cells add up in series.

See ELECTRICITY AND MAGNETISM in volume 18

of the Macropaedia; also under ELECTRIC CATFISH and ELECTRIC EEL in the Micropaedia.

Is it possible to see a black hole?

A black hole is the name given to the volume surrounding a collapsed star (an enormous mass in a tiny space), in which the gravitational field is so large that no radiation can get out; as a result it cannot be seen from outside. The astronomical search for a black hole is made difficult because of the very short time required for their formation (fractions of a second) and the relative infrequency of their creation. After being formed they emit no radiation or signals for the astronomer to detect.

Present efforts are concentrated on the possibility of detecting a gravitational hole with a visible companion binary star. The gravitational wave pulses believed to be detected by the hundreds per year may be the gravitational radiation that would result from massive bodies being strongly accelerated into a large black hole (of thousands of solar masses) located near the centre of the Galaxy.

See GRAVITATION in volume 20 of the Macropaedia.

Where did William Blake see angels?

Poet, painter, engraver, and visionary, William Blake is now seen to have possessed a mind of outstanding originality. Yet he was ignored by the public of his day. He was called mad because he was single-minded and unworldly, and he lived on the edge of poverty.

Blake was born in 1757 in London, then a small city surrounded by villages and fields with market gardens. Blake was brought up in central London, unlike most English poets before him who grew up in the countryside. In later life he recalled the pleasures of rambles in the villages outside London. On one such walk, to Peckham Rye, before he was ten years old, he had a vision in which he saw a tree full of angels. Blake all his life had a strongly visual mind; whatever he imagined, he also saw. He is thought to have had what is now called eidetic imagery – *i.e.* the rare ability to see mental images as if they are suspended outside the head, so that they can be inspected like solid figures by shifting one's gaze from one side to the other. Blake's poetry is charged with the almost physical presence of such images.

See the article on BLAKE in volume 2 of the Micropaedia.

When was blood transfusion first tried?

William Harvey announced his observations on the circulation of the blood in 1616. The discovery that blood circulates around the body in a closed system was an essential prerequisite to the concept of transfusing blood from one animal to another. In England experiments on the transfusion of blood were pioneered in dogs in 1665 by Richard Lower. In 1667 Lower transfused the blood of a lamb into a man – an event recorded in Samuel Pepys' diary. In 1668 Jean-Baptiste Denis, a French experimenter, was arrested after a fatal accident involving the transfusion of lambs' blood into humans. After this little advance was made for 150 years.

The dangers of transfusing blood from other animals to man were established scientifically in the 1870s. The ABO blood groups were discovered in 1900, thus opening the way to safe transfusion procedures.

See BLOOD in volume 15 of the Macropaedia.

How do some animals survive without bones?

In addition to its supportive function, the animal skeleton may provide protection, facilitate movement, and aid in certain sensory functions. Support of the body in many Protozoa is achieved by a simple, stiff, translucent, non-living envelope called a pellicle. In coral, where colonies attain great size, it is achieved by dead structures, both internal and external. Many animals remain erect or in their normal resting position by means of hydrostatic skeleton; *i.e.*, fluid pressure in a confined space. In insects, spiders, and crabs, it is achieved by a cuticle made up of both exoskeletal (external) and endoskeletal (internal) units.

See SUPPORTIVE AND CONNECTIVE TISSUES in volume 28 of the Macropaedia.

How did botanical gardens begin?

The first botanical gardens were centres for the raising of fruit trees, vegetables, and herbs used in making medicines. After the discovery of printing, manuscripts on plants became more widely circulated, and these stimulated further publication of descriptive works called herbals. The herbalists and herbals, in turn, stimulated the founding of botanical gardens. By the end of the 16th century there were five such gardens in Europe. The first two were in Italy, at Padua and Pisa (1545). At first, such gardens were associated with the medical schools of universities. Professors of medicine were mainly the botanists of that time, and their "physic gardens" served for the training of students as well as for growing plants to make medicines.

See BOTANICAL GARDEN in volume 2 of the Micropaedia.

Have men bigger brains than women?

The weight of the human brain varies with age, stature, body weight, sex, and race. When compared to average body stature and weight, the size and weight of the brain in the two sexes are proportionately equal. The brain, which weighs about 380 grams at birth, grows rapidly during the first three years of life and approaches its mature weight at about the seventh year; after this the increase is very gradual. The average weight in males – about 1,400 grams – is attained by the 20th year and in females – about 1,260 grams – somewhat earlier. From this period onward, in both sexes, there is a continuous decrease in the average weight of approximately one gram per year. The cerebrum in humans, the centre of thought and conscious activity, has grown over the rest of the brain forming a convoluted layer of grey matter, and accounts for about 85% of the brain's weight.

See BRAIN in volume 2 of the Micropaedia.

What connects bread and beer?

Brewing and baking were closely connected in early civilizations. Fermentation of a thick gruel resulted in a dough suitable for baking; a thinner mash produced a kind of beer. Both techniques required knowledge of the "mysteries" of fermentation and a supply of grain. Increasing knowledge and experience taught the artisans in the baking and brewing trades that barley was best suited to brewing, while wheat was best for baking.

The phenomenon of fermentation with the resultant lightening of the loaf structure and development of appealing flavours, was probably first observed when doughs or gruels, held for several hours before baking, exhibited spoilage caused by yeasts. Most doughs exhibit some response to the puffing or leavening action of fermentation, but only wheat yields a flour producing a light, porous structure in baked products. Early baked products were made of mixed seeds with a predominance of barley, but wheat flour, because of its superior response to fermentation, eventually became the preferred cereal among cultural groups sufficiently advanced in culinary techniques to make leavened bread.

See FOOD PROCESSING in volume 19 of the Macropaedia.

When was the first British Empire?

During the later imperial period of Rome, Britain for a short period became a separate empire through the rebellion in 286/287 AD of Carausius. This man had commanded against the Saxon pirates in the Channel and by his naval power was able to maintain his independence. At first he sought recognition as co-emperor, but this was refused; in 293 the fall of Boulogne to Roman forces led to his murder and the accession of Allectus, who fell in his turn when Constantius I invaded Britain in 296.

Constantius reformed the administration, and the 4th century was a period of great prosperity throughout Britain. There were ominous withdrawals of troops, however, and when in 407 Constantius III was declared emperor by the army in Britain and took further troops to Gaul, there were no longer sufficient forces on the island to protect it from increasing Pictish and Saxon raids. The legitimate emperor, Honorius, authorized the cities to provide for their own defense. This marks the end of Roman Britain.

Power fell gradually into the hands of tyrants. Chief of these was Vortigern but he, unlike earlier usurpers, made no attempt to become Roman emperor. Independence was producing separate interests.

See UNITED KINGDOM in volume 29 of the Macropaedia.

Whose theories and experiments made him "father of British aeronautics"?

Throughout the years, the conflicting claims of inventors to priority have plagued aviation historians. On one point, however, there is clear consensus. The title of "father of British aeronautics" and, in fact, of all aeronautics rests with Sir George Cayley.

It is true that Leonardo had sketched wing-flapping devices and even a form of helicopter (*c.* 1500), and kites in many forms were commonplace prior to the 17th century. Also the records of the 18th century contain accounts of many weird and wonderful machines for mechanical man flight. But at that time, as always, men's dreams far exceeded their scientific and technical capabilities.

Cayley's active interest in man flight spanned the years from 1792 to his death in 1857. A perceptive theorist and an active experimenter with models and with full-scale gliders, he eventually had at his disposal all the aerodynamic theory required for the design of a man-carrying airplane. The problem, as he saw it, was "to make a surface support a given weight by the application of sufficient power to overcome the resistance of the air." Unfortunately, no light-weight, self-contained power plant was then available. That vital component was still half a century away.

See TRANSPORTATION in volume 28 of the Macropaedia.

What is the largest structure ever built by living creatures?

The Great Barrier Reef. This reef extends for some 2,000 kilometres off the northeastern coast of Australia.

The reef actually consists of some thousands of individual reefs, many dry or barely awash at low tide, some with islands of coral sand, or cays, others fringing high islands or the mainland coast. The reefs share a common origin: each has been formed, over millions of years, from the skeletons and skeletal waste of a mass of living marine organisms. The "bricks" in the reef framework are formed by the calcareous remains of the tiny creatures known as coral polyps and hydrocorals, while the "cement" that binds these remains together is formed in large part by the remains of the organisms known as coralline algae and polyzoas. The interstices of this framework have been filled in by vast quantities of skeletal waste produced by the pounding of the waves and the depredations of boring organisms.

See GREAT BARRIER REEF in volume 5 of the Micropaedia.

What were the first carpets?

Prehistoric man may have happened upon a method of forming thread from twisted grass or hair. Evidence obtained from recent excavations near the Caspian Sea indicates that the shearing of sheep and goats, and the spinning and weaving of the fibres obtained, was practised as early as 6000 BC. Before the development of weaving, fibres were probably interlaced to produce a simple form of plaited basket-work matting, replacing still earlier crude mats made of strands of dry stalks and tendrils.

Findings in burial mounds at Pazyryk in southern Siberia, 2,400 years old, indicate that furs, leather, woven textiles, and felts were used, not as floor coverings, but as wall hangings. The first true carpets, characterized by pile surfaces, were probably rough cured skins that early hunters laid on the floors of their crude dwellings. Most carpets still retain the same tough flexible backings and upright pile, affording protection from cold and hard floors, agreeable to the touch, and serving a decorative function.

Smooth floorings also have ancient origins. In the Late Bronze Age (1600–1000 BC) water-worn pebbles were laid as flooring in Crete and also on the Greek mainland. The Greeks refined the technique between the 6th and the 4th centuries BC, and ancient decorative pebble mosaics have been found in Greece, Asia Minor, and Sicily.

See MANUFACTURING INDUSTRIES in volume 21 of the Macropaedia.

Will there one day be driverless cars?

Increasing efforts are being put forward on many levels in all of the developed countries to untangle the urban transportation problem.

Of the many directions of current research, perhaps that of the most immediate interest is the automatically controlled vehicle. One imaginative concept involves completely relieving the driver of responsibility, substituting an electronic roadway control connected to a central computer system. The principal aim would be to increase safety.

Another version, designed to eliminate the problem of city-centre parking, would provide an army of small vehicles that would be automatically controlled once the destination was identified. So ambitious a system would probably only be feasible, even when technical problems are solved, within a new city that can be designed with the system in mind, or within an area of large-scale reconstruction.

The most important requirement for urban transportation in the 1980s remains funds for research and development. The cost of developing a system capable of meeting the needs of today's congested, pollution-plagued metropolis is fully comparable to that of a major space program.

See TRANSPORTATION in volume 28 of the Macropaedia.

What paints did cave artists use?

Cave paintings in Europe probably date from 20,000–15,000 BC. The colours were rubbed across rock walls and ceilings with sharpened solid lumps of natural earths (yellow, red, and brown ochre). Outlines were drawn with black sticks of charcoal. Mixing dishes found in caves suggest that liquid pigment mixed with fat was also used and smeared with the hand. Subtle colour tones on animals painted in the Altamira and Lascaux caves appear to have been dabbed with fur pads. Feathers and frayed twigs may have been used in painting manes and tails.

The pigments in cave paintings have probably been preserved by a natural process of rainwater seeping through the limestone rocks. Among the earliest images are imprinted and stencilled hands. Paintings from the Magdalenian period (*c.* 10,000 BC) show astonishing powers of observation. Women, warriors, horses, bison and other animals are depicted in scenes of ritual ceremony, battle, and hunting.

See PAINTING, ART OF in volume 25 of the Macropaedia.

Which sage of Chelm was the wiser?

The droll tales of the wise men of Chelm (in Poland) are Jewish counterparts of the German noodles (stupid people) of Schildburg and of the more familiar English wise men of Gotham.

Typical of them is the tale of the two sages who went for a walk, one carrying an umbrella and the other without one. Suddenly it began to rain. "Open your umbrella," said the one without one. "It won't help," answered the other, "it's full of holes." "Then why did you bring it?" rejoined his friend. "I didn't think it would rain," was the reply.

See JUDAISM in volume 22 of the Macropaedia.

How much bigger are children today than children of yesteryear?

During the last 50 to 100 years children have been maturing in the physiological sense at progressively earlier ages. This is likely to become a worldwide phenomenon as nations become more prosperous. In some societies it seems that children reach puberty five years earlier than they did a century ago. The European mean average for menarche (first menstrual period) in girls is now 13·3, with American girls a step or two ahead. Only the Bundi of New Guinea, with an average menarche age of 18·8, are comparable to Europeans of a century ago.

Records kept in schools and clinics suggest that children since about 1900 have on average increased in height, at age five to seven, by one to two centimetres each decade and at 10 to 14, by two to three centimetres each decade. Body weight has also gone up proportionately.

The reasons are probably both genetic and environmental, with better diet and nutrition clearly the most important. Earlier physical maturity has obvious social implications with regard to the age of marriage, for example, and changes in teaching methods to meet the new levels of maturity of pupils. For parents, it may mean that older disciplinary sanctions become less effective; simple veto or moral exhortation no longer going unchallenged.

See SOCIAL DIFFERENTATION in volume 27 of the Macropaedia.

How big is China?

China is the largest of all Asian countries and has the largest population of any country in the world. It covers an area of 9,560,900 square kilometres, which is approximately $\frac{1}{14}$ of the land area of the world. Among the major countries of the world, it is surpassed in area only by the Soviet Union and Canada, and it is larger than either the United States or Brazil. There is one Chinese for every four persons of any other nationality. Both in area and in population, Europe (excluding the Soviet Union) is only half the size of China.

See CHINA in volume 16 of the Macropaedia.

How seaworthy is the Chinese junk?

Compared to some of its Western contemporaries (such as the Viking longship) the Chinese junk appears unwieldy and strange to Western eyes. Yet it is one of the most efficient vessels under sail. Nobody knows how long junks have sailed the Far Eastern seas, but they were making prosperous voyages to India in the 9th century

and through the Middle Ages Chinese merchantmen sailed regularly to the east coast of Africa and even Aden. In 1848 a junk gave a demonstration of its seaworthiness by sailing from China to Boston, New York, and London.

There are, or were, 70 or more different types of junk, some ocean-going, others designed for river traffic. The number of masts varies from one to five (though five is uncommon). There is no keel, but the massive rudder is deep enough to act as a centreboard and reduce drifting. Unique to the junk was the watertight compartment, an idea not adopted in the west for centuries. The square lugsail is made of a series of matting or linen panels, each stiffened by a bamboo batten, with its own sheet leading to the main sheet. Thus, all parts of the sail can be close-hauled, enabling the junk to sail very close to the wind.

The Japanese junk, now rare, is quite different. There is only one type, squat and heavy, and the sails have no bamboo panels.

See TRANSPORTATION in volume 28 of the Macropaedia.

Who smoked the first cigarette?

The Aztecs smoked a hollow reed or cane tube stuffed with tobacco. Other natives of Mexico, Central America, and parts of South America crushed tobacco leaves and rolled the shreds in maize husk or other vegetable wrappers. But it was the cigar rather than this prototype of the cigarette that the conquistadors brought back to Spain as a luxury for the wealthy.

Early in the 16th century beggars in Seville began to pick up discarded cigar butts and roll them in scraps of paper for smoking, thus improvising the first cigarette. Late in the 18th century they acquired respectability and their use spread to Italy and Portugal. They were carried by Portuguese traders to the Levant and Russia, where during the Napoleonic wars, French and British troops became familiar with them. The French named them cigarettes. Forty years later, the Crimean War brought a new generation of soldiers into contact with Turkish cigarettes.

See CIGARETTE in volume 3 of the Micropaedia.

How did circuses begin?

Although some may argue that the recognizable beginnings of the circus may be found as far back as the ancient Greek hippodrome, its origin is usually traced to the circuses and amphitheatres of ancient Rome. Both the Roman circuses and amphitheatres, however, were designed for horse racing or for spectacles intended to end fatally for either man or beast – the opposite of the displays of cooperation that are the essence of the circus today.

There were no organized circuses during the Middle Ages, but tumblers, jugglers, acrobats, actors, and dancers wandered individually or in groups through Europe, Asia, and Africa. They appeared wherever people gathered, in nobles' halls, at celebrations, and at market places.

The modern circus came into being in England, in 1768, when Philip Astley, a former sergeant major turned trick rider, found that if he galloped in a circle while standing on his horse's back, centrifugal force helped him to keep his balance. In doing so he traced the first ring. The name circus was first used in 1782 when the Royal Circus was set up near Astley's by Charles Hughes, one of Astley's horsemen.

See PAGEANTRY AND SPECTACLE in volume 25 of the Macropaedia.

How is cold used in surgery?

Cryosurgery is surgery performed with a freezing probe instead of a cutting edge.

Freezing an aqueous solution, such as the content of a living cell, is a dehydration process. As water is converted to ice, the solutes present become more concentrated, until precipitation occurs. In a cell or tissue the dissolved colloids are subjected to increasing concentrations of electrolytes such as salt. Base-acid changes may occur, with the concentration of components contributing to the concentration of the hydrogen ion. The normal spatial arrangements of subcellular components may be disrupted by the volume change during expansion. All these and other phenomena introduce irreversible changes that can destroy the viability of a cell.

Even though very low temperatures can destroy life, when selective tissue destruction is the end sought, as in surgery, cryogenics becomes a useful tool in well-being and in the prolongation of life. Cryogenic surgical treatment prevents bleeding and widespread tissue damage.

See REFRIGERATION in volume 26 of the Macropaedia.

How do you conduct without a baton?

At the most fundamental level, a conductor must stress the musical pulse so that all the performers can follow the same metrical rhythm. Traditionally conductors have held a baton in the right hand as a device for emphasizing the metrical outline, reserving the left hand for indicating entries of different parts and nuances. Many contemporary conductors, however, follow a practice long established in unaccompanied choral conducting and dispense with the baton; present-day performers are generally too knowledgeable to need this extra visual guide, and its absence frees both hands for more elaborately interpretive directions.

With the removal of the baton and, through memorization, the elimination of the printed score in public performance, the conductor is free to use not only his hands and arms but also the movement of his torso and facial muscles to express to the group his wishes in the execution of phrasing, dynamic level, nuance, individual entrances, and other aspects of a finished performance.

The most effective 20th-century conductors have been glamorous, gifted musicians and skilled technocrats, capable of dealing authoritatively with professionals in their own field.

See CONDUCTING in volume 3 of the Micropaedia.

Which conquistador had to stow away to escape his creditors?

Vasco Núñez de Balboa, Spanish conquistador and explorer, was the first European discoverer of the Pacific Ocean. In 1500 he sailed on a voyage of exploration along the coast of present-day Colombia. Later, he settled in Hispaniola (Haiti), but he did not prosper as a pioneer farmer and had to escape his creditors by embarking as a stowaway on another Spanish expedition.

The Spaniards went on to found the town of Santa Maria de la Antigua on the isthmus of Panama. There they began to acquire gold by barter or war with the local Indians. They were told by the Indians that to the south lay a sea and a province infinitely rich in gold – a reference to the Pacific and perhaps to the Inca Empire. Accompanied by 190 Spaniards and hundreds of Indian carriers, Balboa marched south across the isthmus through dense jungles, rivers, and swamps and ascended the cordillera; on September 25 (or 27), 1513, "Silent, upon a peak in Darien", he sighted the Pacific.

See the article on BALBOA in volume 1 of the Micropaedia.

Do the continents move?

The sea-floor spreading hypothesis was proposed in 1960 by the American geo-physicist Harry H. Hess. On the basis of new discoveries about the deep-ocean floor, Hess postulated that molten material from the earth's mantle continuously wells up along the crests of the mid-ocean ridges that wind for 60,000 kilometres through all the world's oceans. As the magma cools, it is pushed away from the sides of the ridges. This spreading creates a successively younger ocean floor, and the flow of material is thought to bring about the migration, or drifting apart, of the continents.

The continents bordering the Atlantic Ocean, for example, are thought to be moving away from the Mid-Atlantic Ridge at a rate of about two centimetres per year, thus increasing the breadth of the ocean basin by twice that amount. Wherever continents are bordered by deep-sea trenches, as in the Pacific Ocean, the ocean floor is believed to plunge downward, underthrusting the continents and ultimately re-entering and dissolving in the deeper levels of the Earth.

See SEA-FLOOR SPREADING in volume 10 of the Micropaedia.

When were cosmetics first used?

It is quite probable that cosmetics had their origin in China, but it is necessary to turn to Egypt for the source of the earliest records of cosmetic substances and their application. Toilet articles and unguent vases have been found in royal tombs dating back to about 3500 BC. According to eyewitnesses at the opening of the tomb of Tutankhamen, who ruled about 1350 BC, the unguent vases contained quantities of aromatics that were still elusively fragrant.

It is probable that the priests made most of these compounds, and their manufacture was considered a mysterious and much honoured art. Arabia supplied the greater proportion of the basic ingredients such as myrrh, frankincense, and spikenard.

Cosmetics were used by Egyptian ladies who enhanced their personal beauty by using somewhat crude paints; Cleopatra's reign saw the zenith of this fashion. The makeup of the eyes received greatest attention, and the results were not unlike some 20th-century makeup effects. The underside of the eye was painted green and the lid, lashes, and eyebrows black by the application of kohl.

See Dress and Adornment in volume 17 of the Macropaedia.

What cricketing controversy was resolved in 1864?

Early in the 19th century, all bowling was underhand, and most bowlers favoured the high tossed lob. The next bowling development was the "round arm revolution", in which many bowlers began raising the point at which they released the ball. Controversy raged furiously, and in 1835 the MCC rephrased the law to allow the hand to be raised as high as the shoulder. Gradually bowlers raised the hand higher in defiance of the law until it became more honoured in the breach than in the observance.

Matters were brought to a head when all nine professionals of an English team playing against Surrey at the Oval left the field in protest at one of their number's being no-balled for throwing (*i.e.* cocking and then, in the release, straightening the arm). As a result, in 1864, the bowler was officially given full liberty to bowl overhand. From time to time umpires have had trouble with bowlers who threw.

See Sports in volume 28 of the Macropaedia.

Does a crocodile's diet include humans?

Crocodiles are predators, mostly nocturnal (*i.e.*, active at night), and spend most of their time in the water; they are also known to take rather long journeys over land. In their first weeks of life crocodiles eat mostly worms and water insects, then frogs and tadpoles; finally, their main diet is fish. Older crocodiles are more apt to prey upon waterfowl and on mammals, and occasionally a member of one of the larger species eats a human. This happens so infrequently, however, that crocodiles cannot be generally regarded as maneaters.

Crocodiles capture water animals in their jaws with a sideways movement of the muzzle. To catch land animals they remain motionless at the edge of a water hole from which the prey habitually drink, or they float passively in the water, resembling a drifting log. With a swift blow of the tail, they knock unsuspecting prey into the water. A number of crocodile species grip the legs of the victim in their jaws, then rotate themselves rapidly, thus tearing the prey apart. When a crocodile cannot consume all of a victim at one time, it drags the carcass into its burrow.

See Reptiles in volume 26 of the Macropaedia.

When did children go on a crusade?

The crusades were military expeditions organized by Western Christians against Muslim powers in order to take possession of or maintain control over the Holy City of Jerusalem and the places associated with the earthly life of Jesus Christ. Between 1095, when the First Crusade was launched, and 1291, when the Latin Christians were finally expelled from their bases in Syria, historians have counted eight major expeditions. Many other lesser ventures also took place.

After the Fourth Crusade (which had been disastrous for the cause of both Christianity and the crusades), there was still to be found something of the original crusading fervour in certain areas of European society. Even children became the victims of mass hysteria, and in 1212, in the so-called Children's Crusade, thousands of youngsters from France and Germany set out to free the Holy Land, only to be lost, shipwrecked, or sold into slavery.

See CRUSADES in volume 16 of the Macropaedia.

How does the cuckoo decide where to lay her egg?

About 50 species of cuckoos are brood parasites – *i.e.* they lay their eggs in the nests of other species, which then rear the young cuckoos.

Many birds react to a foreign object in the nest by deserting the nest, building another nest on top of the first, or removing the offending object. It is therefore of great advantage to a brood parasite to lay eggs that resemble those of its host. But the utilization of several host species by a single population of cuckoos presents a difficult adaptive problem, for the host species may have many different egg colours.

Each female common cuckoo lays eggs of a particular shape and coloration throughout her life, but the eggs of different females vary widely. Most authorities now agree that a female normally restricts her parasitism to the single host species by which she herself was reared, and that the common cuckoo population is composed of numerous clans, called gentes, each of which parasitizes only one species of bird, for which the females of that gente have evolved egg mimicry.

Only the gente of the female is important in egg coloration; the foster parentage of the male (*i.e.* his gente) has no effect on his choice of females, and his genetic makeup apparently does not influence the coloration of eggs laid by his female offspring. Gentes are sometimes known by their host species ("redstart cuckoo", "dunnock cuckoo", etc.). Evidence for this theory is largely circumstantial but no plausible alternative theory has been proposed.

See BIRDS in volume 15 of the Macropaedia.

How did Dada choose its name?

The Dada movement was a nihilistic movement in the arts that flourished primarily in Zürich, New York, Berlin, Cologne, Hannover, and Paris in the early 20th century. Several explanations have been given by various members of the movement as to how it received its name. According to the most widely accepted account, the name was adopted at Hugo Ball's Cabaret Voltaire, in Zürich, during one of the meetings held in 1916 by a group of young artists and war resistors, which included Jean Arp, Richard Hülsenbeck, Tristan Tzara, Marcel Janco, and Emmy Hennings. When a paper knife inserted into a French–German dictionary pointed to the word *dada* (French word for hobbyhorse), this word was seized upon as an appropriate name for their anti-aesthetic creations and protest activities, engendered by disgust for bourgeois values and despair over World War I.

See DADA in volume 3 of the Micropaedia.

What was the Dance of Death?

Also called the *danse macabre*, the dance of death was a medieval allegorical concept of the all-consuming and equalizing power of death, expressed in a literary or pictorial representation of a procession or dance of both living and dead figures. The living were arranged in order of their rank, from pope and emperor to child, clerk, and hermit, with the dead leading them all to their grave. The medieval obsession with death inspired by the Black Death and the devastation of the Hundred Years' War (1337–1453) made the dance of death a frequent theme in monastery and church decoration north of the Alps.

The concept of the dance of death lost its awesome hold in the Renaissance, but the universality of its theme inspired its revival in Romantic literature and in 19th and 20th century music. In 1956 it was effectively used as the visual climax of Ingmar Bergman's film *The Seventh Seal*.

See DANCE OF DEATH in volume 3 of the Micropaedia.

What was a "deus ex machina"?

Stage properties and decoration during the first period of the Greek theatre were very simple; the backdrop was originally a temporary wooden skeleton covered with screens of animal skins painted red. It was not until Aeschylus that canvases were decorated according to the needs of a particular play. Aristotle credits Sophocles with the invention of scene-painting, an innovation ascribed by others to Aeschylus.

By the latter part of the 5th century, scene-changing was accomplished by the use of moveable painted screens. By this time the *machina* or flying machine was an important stage property. Evidence for its use can be found in the comedies of Aristophanes; a character in his play *Peace* ascends to heaven on a dung beetle and appeals to the scene shifter not to let him fall. In the time of Euripedes, the *machina* was used conventionally for the epilogue. At that point the crane was used so that a god could descend from heaven to sort out the complications in the plot at the end of a tragedy, a convention that became known as a *deus ex machina* – "god from a machine". The lavish use of flying machines is testified to by the poet Antiphanes, who wrote that tragic playwrights lift up a machine as readily as they lift a finger when they do not have anything to say.

See THEATRICAL PRODUCTION in volume 28 of the Macropaedia.

What was the Black Dog of Winchester?

A monstrous goblin dog, with huge teeth and claws, appears in the folklore of much of England and Wales. It was thought that those who saw one clearly would die soon after, while those who only caught a glimpse of the beast would live on, but only for some months. The Barghest of Yorkshire, the Demon of Tidworth, the Black Dog of Winchester, and the Padfoot of Wakefield are all related apparitions. Their Welsh counterparts were red-eyed Gwyllgi, the Dog of Darkness, and Cwn Annwn, the Dogs of Hell. In Lancashire the dog was called Trash, Skriker, or Striker; its broad, sometimes backward-pointing feet made a splashing noise, and it howled horribly. In East Anglia, where it was thought to be amphibious, the dog had only one eye and was known as Black Shuck or Shock. The Manchester Barghest was said to be headless.

See BARGHEST in volume 1 of the Micropaedia.

Should dreams come true?

In some cultures, dream events are believed to demand fulfillment. Jesuit priests in the 1700s reported that among Iroquois Indians it was obligatory to carry out dreams as soon as possible; one Indian was said to have dreamed that ten friends dived into a hole in the ice and came up through another. When told of the dream, the friends duly enacted their roles in it, but unfortunately only nine of them succeeded.

After dreaming of something valuable, Kurdish people were immediately expected to take it, by force if necessary. Among some natives of Kamchatka a man need only dream of a girl's favour for her to owe him her sexual favours.

See SLEEP AND DREAMS in volume 27 of the Macropaedia.

How powerful is dust?

Dust may be carried by the wind for thousands of kilometres. Dust from North Africa falls in England, 3,200 kilometres away, and Australian dust is blown a similar distance to New Zealand. Dust thrown high into the atmosphere by volcanoes can circle the globe several times. Individual storms carry as much as 100 million tons of dust.

Wind-driven sand has a powerful abrasive effect – as power and telephone companies know. The wires of a low-strung Trans-Caspian phone

line are reported to have lost half their diameter within a decade. This abrasiveness is put to use in sandblasting cleaning, an efficient technique for cleaning dirty buildings or etching decorative concrete.

See GEOMORPHIC PROCESSES in volume 20 of the Macropaedia.

Who made the first earthquake recorder?

Ancient accounts of earthquakes are sometimes valuable as historical records but tell little about the causes of these events. Aristotle held that volcanic explosions and earthquakes alike are caused by spasmodic motions of hot winds that move underground and occasionally burst forth. The Chinese have the double distinction of keeping the most faithful records of their earthquakes and of inventing the first instrument capable of detecting them. Records of major quakes in China go back to 780 BC.

In order to detect quakes at a distance, the mathematician, astronomer, and geographer Chang Heng (AD 78–139) invented an instrument that has been called the first seismograph. It consisted of a large bronze vessel containing a heavy pendulum. Arms radiating in eight directions of the compass were levered in the walls of the vessel so that they could be moved by the first swing of the pendulum. When the pendulum was set in motion by earthquake waves, one or another of the arms would be moved, releasing a bronze ball that would fall into a cup attached to the bottom of the vessel. When this happened, the pendulum was immobilized. The position of the ball that had fallen permitted an estimation of the direction from which the quake had come.

See EARTH SCIENCES in volume 17 of the Macropaedia.

Who discovered Easter Island?

Easter Island, now a Chilean dependency, is an island in the eastern Pacific. It is famous for its stone statues, of which there are more than 600, and for the ruins of giant stone platforms, which show masterly construction. The sizes of some of the statues reach stupendous proportions. Experiments have shown that 180 persons were needed to pull a medium-sized statue over the ground.

The first European to land on Easter Island was the Dutch admiral Jacob Roggeveen, who paid it a single day's visit in 1722. He found a racially mixed population worshipping in front of huge standing statues. In 1770 a Spanish expedition reported a population of between 900 and 3,000, but when the English navigator Captain Cook arrived in 1774 a decimated, poverty-stricken population of only about 600 or 700 men and less than 30 women was found. The statues were no longer venerated, most of them having been deliberately overthrown, apparently during a civil war. Slavery and a smallpox epidemic further reduced the population of Easter Island to 111 before at the end of the last century it began to increase once more.

See PACIFIC ISLANDS in volume 25 of the Macropaedia.

Who is generally held to be the father of economics?

No-one has ever succeded in neatly defining the scope of economics. It is easier to indicate what economists do. Among other things, they seek to analyze the forces determining prices – not only the prices of goods and services but the prices of the resources used to produce them. Microeconomics deals with the behaviour of individuals (consumers, business firms, farmers, and so on). Macroeconomics deals with aggregates: the level of income in the whole economy, the volume of total employment and so on.

The effective birth of economics may be traced to the year 1776 when Adam Smith published *An Inquiry into the Nature and Causes of the Wealth of Nations*. There was, of course, economics before Adam Smith. But his book, the first full-scale treatise, founded what later generations were to call the "English School of Classical Political Economy".

In the 19th century economics was the hobby of gentlemen of leisure. Economists were rarely consulted by government. Today there are perhaps 20,000 or more economists in the world – their numbers have never been accurately counted. And the number grows about 5 per cent a year. This is indeed "the age of economists".

See SOCIAL SCIENCES in volume 27 of the Macropaedia.

Where did eggs once cost $1 apiece?

In 1846, when it was captured by the Americans, the Californian settlement of Yerba Buena had a total population of 460. The next year it was renamed San Francisco.

With the discovery of gold, San Francisco

picked up pace and direction. The modest village was almost deserted at first as its population scrambled inland to the Mother Lode, and then it exploded into one of the most extraordinary cities ever built. Some 40,000 gold hunters arrived by sea, another 30,000 plodded across the Great Basin, and still another 9,000 moved north from Mexico. By 1851 more than 800 ships rode at anchor in the harbour, deserted by their crews.

Everybody except the miners got rich. Eggs sold for $1 apiece, and downtown real estate prices could almost have held their own against the appreciated values of the late 20th century. Until the bubble burst in the Panic of 1857, 50,000 San Franciscans became rich and went bankrupt, cheated and swindled one another, and took to the pistol and knife all too readily. As the *Sacramento Union* noted in 1856, there had been "some fourteen hundred murders in San Francisco in six years, and only three of the murderers hung, and one of these was a friendless Mexican."

In 1859, silver was discovered in the Nevada Territory, and the exploitation of the Comstock Lode, which eventually yielded $300,000,000, turned San Francisco from a frontier boom town into a metropolis whose leading citizens were bankers, speculators, and lawyers, whose women dressed in Paris gowns and who ate and drank in splendid hotels and restaurants.

The 1860s and 1870s marked the birth of the modern San Francisco, which has for more than a hundred years laid claim with some justice to being the Athens, Paris, and New York of the West, but which never completely lost the mark of its wild beginning. As Rudyard Kipling was to observe when he visited the city in the 1890s, "San Francisco is a mad city, inhabited for the most part by perfectly insane people, whose women are of remarkable beauty."

See San Francisco in volume 27 of the Macropaedia.

What three principles are the basis of the electrical power industry?

1. An electric current flowing along a wire generates a magnetic field in the space around the wire. The strength of this field is proportional to the size of the current and diminishes as the distance from the wire increases. The field can be made strongest by winding the wire into a coil of many turns and can be concentrated in space by filling the volume inside the coil with iron, thus creating a device known as an electro-magnet, in which the magnetic field can be controlled by adjusting the size of the current flowing in the coil.

2. When placed in a magnetic field, a wire carrying an electric current experiences a mechanical force. The magnetic field may be generated by a permanent magnet or, more commonly, by a second coil also carrying an electric current. Magnetic forces provide the fundamental motive power in electromagnetic machinery; powerful forces can be generated by comparatively small machines and be conveniently controlled by adjustment of the size of the currents.

3. When a coil of wire is situated in a magnetic field that is increasing or decreasing, an electrical voltage proportional to the rate of change of the field is created in the coil. This is the phenomenon of electromagnetic induction that forms the basis of the dynamo. A coil rotated in a magnetic field generates an alternating voltage, and an alternating current (ac) flows if the coil is connected to a continuous electrical circuit. By a special arrangement of connections to the rotating coil, it is possible to draw direct current (dc) instead of alternating current from the coil.

See Electricity and Magnetism in volume 18 of the Macropaedia.

When was the electric car invented?

Invention of the storage battery, by Gaston Planté of France in 1859–60, and its improvement by Camille Faure in 1881 made the electric vehicle possible; and what was probably the first, a tricycle, ran in Paris in 1881. It was followed by other three-wheelers in London, 1882, and Boston, 1888. The first American battery-powered automobile, built in Des Moines, Iowa, in 1890, could maintain a speed of 23 kilometres per hour.

At the turn of the century, 38 percent of the automobiles in the United States, the country in which the electric car had maximum acceptance, were powered by electricity. (40 percent were powered by steam and 22 percent by gasoline.) It was another application of battery power, the electric self-starter, that did as much as anything to doom the electric car by eliminating the dreaded hand crank.

See Transportation in volume 28 of the Macropaedia.

Who first described electromagnetism?

Although the properties of magnets had been known centuries before, the father of the modern subject of electromagnetism was William Gilbert (1544–1603). In a book published three years before his death, he not only discussed magnetism, especially the magnetism of the Earth, but also considered the force between two objects charged by friction. To this force he gave the name electric.

Gilbert attributed the electrification of a body by friction to the removal of a fluid or "humour" which then left an "effluvium" around the body. The language is quaint but if the "humour" is renamed "charge" and the "effluvium" renamed "electric field", Gilbert's notions closely approached modern ideas.

See ELECTRICITY AND MAGNETISM in volume 18 of the Macropaedia.

What is the difference between chemical elements, compounds, and mixtures?

Chemical elements are the fundamental materials of which all matter is composed. From the modern viewpoint, a substance that cannot be decomposed into simpler substances by ordinary chemical processes is, by definition, an element.

Elements can combine with one another to form a wide variety of more complex substances called compounds. The number of possible compounds is almost infinite; perhaps a million are known, and more are being discovered every day. When two or more elements combine to form a compound, they lose their separate identities, and the product has characteristics quite different from those of the constituent elements. The gaseous elements hydrogen and oxygen, for example, with quite different properties, can combine to form the compound water, which has altogether different properties from either oxygen or hydrogen.

Mixtures differ from compounds in that they can be separated into their component parts by physical processes; for example, the simple process of evaporation separates water from the other compounds in seawater.

See CHEMICAL ELEMENTS in volume 15 of the Macropaedia.

Where was the first passenger elevator installed?

The practice of lifting loads by mechanical means goes back at least to Roman times. Lifting platforms for building operations used pulleys and capstans operated by human, animal, or water power. Steam power was applied to such devices in England by 1800 and in the early 19th century the first hydraulic lift was introduced. All these devices employed counter-weights to balance the weight of the car, requiring only enough power to raise the load.

However, the poor reliability of the ropes (generally hemp) used at that time made such lifts unsatisfactory for passengers. In 1853 an American, Elisha Graves Otis, introduced a new safety device – a clamping arrangement which gripped the guide rails on which the car moved when tension was released from the hoist rope. This made possible the passenger lift or elevator; the first was put into service at the Haughwout Department Store in New York City in 1857. Driven by steam power, it climbed five stories in less than a minute. The first electrically operated passenger lift appeared in 1889, push-button controls following five years later.

See ELEVATOR in volume 4 of the Micropaedia.

Does England really exist?

England is the predominant part of the United Kingdom, yet constitutionally no longer exists. It is not mentioned in the title of its sovereign. England does not have its own set of official

statistics, and in its institutions, it gives the appearance of having been swallowed up in the larger mass of the United Kingdom since the Act of Union of 1707. It sometimes seems that Scotland and Wales have been more successful in retaining or securing their own special institutions. The "Englishness" of England is a quality hard to define, yet there is no doubt that it exists. Most institutions are British, but poets have very rarely saluted Britain. (One exception is Britannia, called on to rule the waves in the patriotic song with words by a Scottish poet.)

See UNITED KINGDOM in volume 29 of the Macropaedia.

What are enzymes?

Practically all of the numerous and complex biochemical reactions that take place in animals, plants, and microorganisms are regulated by enzymes. The word enzyme comes from the Greek meaning "in yeast"; their existence was discovered in the middle of the 19th century by scientists studying the process of fermentation.

Enzymes play an important role in metabolism. Some help to break down large nutrient molecules, such as proteins, fats, and carbohydrates, into smaller molecules: this occurs during digestion in the stomach and intestines of animals. Others guide these smaller molecules through the intestinal wall into the bloodstream. Still others promote the formation of large complex molecules from the small, simple ones during the creation of cells. Enzymes are responsible for numerous other functions, which include the storage and release of energy, the course of reproduction, the processes of respiration, and vision. They are indispensible to life.

See BIOLOGICAL COMPONENTS OF ORGANISMS in volume 14 of the Macropaedia.

Where would you find ergs?

Ergs are areas of continuous sands, long considered a typical feature of the Sahara Desert (although they cover only about 20 percent of its surface). Within the ergs, pyramid-shaped dunes are formed. In the wind, the sand "smokes" and a drumming is heard, called the Spirit of Raoul, the drummer of death. In parts of the Sahara, erosional forces have produced fantastic rock formations. In the sandstone regions, "ghost castles", grotesque "mountains", and forests of stone pillars seem tossed about in confusion. On the plains, petrified trees are found, half buried in the sand. Wandering sand masses threaten settlements, and sandstorms and dust clouds hinder travel.

The Sahara is the world's largest tropical and climatic desert, with an area of 8,600,000 square kilometres. In the south, known in Arabic as the *sahel*, the desert is slowly encroaching. Almost as large as the United States, the Sahara has only about 2,000,000 inhabitants. Huge areas are wholly empty. Yet long before recorded history, the desert was evidently more fertile and more widely occupied by man. Almost all ergs are rich in relics of the Stone Age, containing fish-hooks on old lake bottoms, pottery, and tombs.

See AFRICA in volume 13 of the Macropaedia.

Who were the Etruscans?

The Etruscans were an ancient people called Tyrsenoi by the Greeks, and Tusci or Etrusci by the Latins or Romans. They called themselves Rasenna. Their country, Etruria in Latin, lay in central Italy between the valley of the Tiber, the valley of the Arno and the Apennines, and Etruscan documents reveal that these people lived there from the beginning of the 7th century BC onwards.

The theory that the Etruscans migrated to Italy from the East is widely accepted by scholars. They may have been Aegean navigators or even the "sea peoples" recorded in Egyptian monuments of the late 13th and early 12th centuries BC. The Etruscan language, the third great language of culture in Italy after Greek and Latin, does not survive in any literary works. Etruscan had already ceased to be spoken in the time of imperial Rome and its surviving writings interested only a few scholars.

The overall picture is that of a nation of navigators, traders, and industrial producers, which underwent a sudden and premature decline in the 5th and 4th centuries BC. After the rise to power of Rome, the Etruscan cities preserved a formal autonomy until 90 BC, when Roman citizenship was given to all the Italic people.

See GRECO–ROMAN CIVILIZATION in volume 20 of the Macropaedia.

Where were explosives discovered?

It may never be known with certainty who invented the first explosive, black powder, which is a mixture of saltpetre (potassium nitrate), sulfur, and charcoal (carbon). The consensus is that it originated in China in the 10th century, but that its use there was almost exclusively in fireworks and signals.

There is, however, some evidence that the Arabs invented black powder. By about 1300, certainly, they had developed the first real gun, a bamboo tube reinforced with iron, which used a charge of black powder to fire an arrow.

A strong case can also be made that black powder was discovered by the English medieval scholar Roger Bacon, who wrote explicit instructions for its preparation in 1242. But Bacon read Arabic, and it is possible that he got his knowledge from Arabic sources.

Nitroglycerin, another chemical explosive, was discovered by an Italian chemist, Ascanio Sobrero, in 1846. It was largely a laboratory curiosity until the Swedish inventor Immanuel Nobel and his son Alfred made extensive studies of its commercial potential in the years 1859–61.

Even today most experts regard Alfred Nobel's invention of the blasting cap, a device for detonating explosives, in 1865, as the greatest advance in the science of explosives since the discovery of black powder.

The second most important of Nobel's inventions was dynamite, in 1867. The basis for the invention was his discovery that kieselguhr, a porous siliceous earth, would absorb large quantities of nitroglycerin, giving a product that was much safer to handle and easier to use than nitroglycerin alone.

See CHEMICAL PROCESS INDUSTRIES in volume 21 of the Macropaedia.

Who liked to be known as "the first farmer of the land"?

George Washington, first president of the United States, was descended from a family which was granted land under Henry VIII. But the family fortunes later fell with the Puritan revolution in England and Washington's great-grandfather emigrated to Virginia in 1657.

The young Washington began his military career in the 1750s when he went on an expedition into the Ohio Valley to combat the French. By then he was already head of the Washington family (his father having died when he was 11, and his mother when he was 20), and so also head of the family estate at Mount Vernon. He always thought farming the "most delectable" of pursuits, declaring it to be "honorable, amusing and, with superior judgement, profitable". He tried to keep abreast of the latest advances in farm techniques and his greatest pride in later days was to be regarded as the nation's first farmer.

See WASHINGTON, GEORGE in volume 29 of the Macropaedia.

Why does one kind of angler fish remain mated for life?

Angler fishes belong to a large order of fishes known as Paracanthopterygii, one of the six major branches of the Teleostei or bony fishes. (The largest of this order are the cod fishes, which may exceed 90 kilograms. Their fecundity is prodigious, females laying many millions of eggs each season.) Less is known about the breeding habits of the deep-sea angler fishes, but it is believed that the eggs float to the surface, the hatched larvae descending to deeper waters as they grow older.

The females of the deep-sea anglers are from three to 13 times as large as the male. In 1922 an angler fish was discovered with small specimens attached to its abdomen. These were thought to be its young. Later, similar finds led to the discovery that the smaller fish were really mature males living as parasites on the female. Soon after their transformation from the larval stage,

the males bite onto an older, larger female. After this, the female and male tissues unite, and the male becomes a permanent appendage of the female.

See FISHES in volume 19 of the Macropaedia.

How are fish found in deep water?

Fish in shallow waters can easily be seen. Even on the high seas, fish can be located when they surface temporarily. Fish searching by direct observation from a vessel is important even today. But in modern times fish, whale, or seal searching is done in many areas by airplanes or helicopters. Identification by species is accomplished by observing the shoal's form or colour or behaviour and sometimes by the presence of accompanying birds. Other animals may also indicate fish concentrations by their presence. Porpoises, for example, are known companions of tuna.

To find fish in deeper waters by other means was difficult if not impossible in the past. Herring fishermen used signal lines. These were long wires dropped from a boat. The fisherman holding the line in his hand could feel the vibration caused by the fish touching the line, which was named the herring's telephone.

One of the most important physical properties for fish finding is the temperature of the water. The use of thermometers was one of the first practices fishermen learned from oceanographers, not only for fish finding but also for forecasting availability of the desired species.

It is possible to judge the vertical distance between the bottom of the ocean and the hull of a vessel by transmitting sound waves and measuring the time required for the reflected wave to return. A shoal of fish registers on such equipment (echo sounder) as an obstacle. An experienced operator can locate fish with an echo sounder and can even judge their quantity. Some fish give typical signals, so that even the species can be identified.

See FISHING AND MARINE PRODUCTS in volume 19 of the Macropaedia.

How do flying fishes fly?

The flying fish (there are actually about 40 species found in warm seas) is a small fish with winglike fins and an unevenly forked tail. It builds up speed underwater and, on breaking the surface, gains additional thrust from rapid beats of the

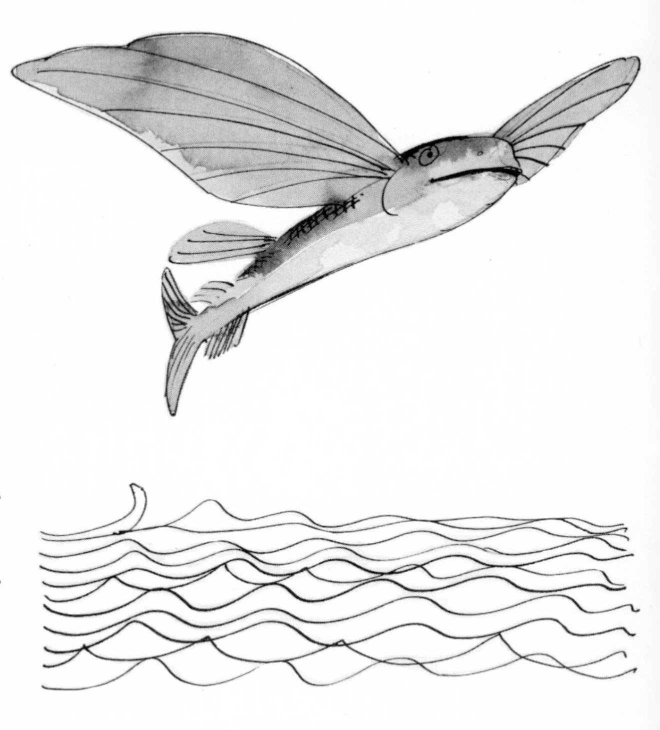

still-submerged tail. The flying fish does not flap its "wings" but glides. Once airborne, it can make several consecutive glides, using its tail each time for extra power.

See FLYING FISH in volume 4 of the Micropaedia.

Why do we forget?

Any theory of forgetting must cope with the primitive observation that forgetting tends to occur when the memory of past experience is not activated for days or months. The fact that different kinds of information are forgotten at different rates must also be accommodated.

It has been suggested that as time passes the physiological bases of memory tend to change. With disuse, it is held that the neural engram (the memory trace in the brain) gradually decays or loses it clarity. While such a theory seems reasonable, decay or deterioration does not seem attributable merely to the passage of time; some underlying physical process needs to be demonstrated.

A major theory of forgetting is anchored in the phenomena of interference. New learning interferes with retention of the old, and conversely, old memories interfere with the retention of new ones. Sources of interference are most pervasive and should not be considered narrowly. For example, any memory seems to be established in specific surroundings or context, and subsequent efforts to remember tend to be less effective when the circumstances differ from the original.

Defect of memory is one of the most frequently observed symptoms of impaired brain function. It may be transitory, after an alcoholic bout or an epileptic seizure; or it may be enduring as after severe head injury or in association with brain disease. Some memory failure is almost universal in old age, particularly in forgetfulness for names and in the reduced ability to learn.

See MEMORY in volume 23 of the Macropaedia.

Who built prefabricated forts?

Military engineering is the oldest of the engineering skills. Evidence of it can be found in Europe in the hill forts constructed by men of the late Iron Age, and also in the Middle East, Africa, and Asia from an early age.

The art of fortifying and of attacking fortified places reached new heights after the fall of the Roman Empire. In 1066 William the Conqueror brought a novel wooden fort, or donjon, from Normandy to England in prefabricated sections to erect on the Hastings beachhead. Later, as he advanced through the country, William built a great number of temporary forts constructed in wood atop a high mound of earth, called a motte, and further protected by an outer ditch and palisade, called a bailey. Such temporary forts were abandoned as permanent stone castles were built to replace them; the motte and bailey design was retained, however.

See THE THEORY AND CONDUCT OF WAR in volume 29 of the Macropaedia.

When will the fossil fuels run out?

Fossil fuels are those organic materials that have been converted from their original form by physical and chemical processes within the Earth's crust into a solid mineral state (coal), a liquid (petroleum), or a gas (natural gas). If these substances are completely burned (oxidized) when used as fuel, the end products are carbon dioxide, water, and heat energy. These cannot be reconstituted into organic substances without either elaborate synthesis in a chemical laboratory or the natural photosynthetic processes of green plants. Thus, burning destroys fossil fuels as a useful energy source available to man.

On the basis of existing knowledge of the amount of fossil fuels in the Earth's crust, it has been predicted that supplies of petroleum and natural gas may be exhausted by 2070 if used at the rates anticipated. Although coal supplies are greater, projected rates of use indicate that they cannot be expected to last for more than a few centuries. These predictions can be changed, of course, if rates of use change, which is expected to happen with, for instance, the further development of nuclear-power sources.

See CONSERVATION OF NATURAL RESOURCES in volume 16 of the Macropaedia.

What did Galileo see through his telescope?

Galileo's telescope used basic optical principles. His first telescope, constructed in a day, magnified three diameters and consisted of a convex lens (curving outward) and a concave lens (curving inward) fitted into opposite ends of a tiny lead tube. The results were so gratifying that Galileo made several larger telescopes, grinding his own lenses. His largest telescope was about 4·4 centimetres in diameter and had a magnifying power of 33 diameters.

With these simple instruments he discovered the mountains and craters of the Moon's surface,

the satellites of Jupiter, the starry nature of the Milky Way, and the fact that Venus undergoes phases like those of the Moon. His observations showed that Venus shines by reflected light, is spherical, and goes round the Sun, contrary to Ptolemaic theory.

These discoveries of Galileo's resulted from two distinct characteristics of a telescope, its magnifying power and its light-gathering power. Rarely has a new scientific instrument had a more dramatic impact. It not only advanced scientific knowledge by enormous strides but stirred vast waves in philosophy and religion by upsetting the traditional picture of a universe centred on a stationary Earth.

See Measurement and Observation in volume 18 of the Macropaedia.

What were gargoyles for?

The first gargoyles were the carved lions of classical cornices or terra-cotta drainage spouts such as those found at Pompeii. In the Gothic period, gargoyles developed into grotesque beasts or birds sitting on the back of a cornice molding and projected forward for several feet in order to throw the water far from the building.

See Gargoyle in volume 5 of the Micropaedia.

What is the main difference between ancient and modern gems?

Since ancient times gems have fascinated mankind. From the early Sumerian period onward, they have been engraved with designs for sealing (intaglio) or for decoration (cameo).

Of decisive significance for the history of modern jewelry was the kind of cutting known as faceting, which produces brilliance by refraction and reflection of light. Until the late Middle Ages gems of all kinds were cut either *en cabochon*, that is rounded, usually with a flat underside, or, for purposes of encrustation, into flat platelets. Faceting can bring about the loss of half the stone or more, but its value is greatly increased.

See Dress and Adornment in volume 17 of the Macropaedia.

How did the Globe Theatre catch fire?

The Globe Theatre was the famous London theatre in which the plays of William Shakespeare were performed after 1599.

The Globe had a thatched gallery roof. In 1613, during a performance of *Henry VIII*, this thatch was accidentally set alight by a cannon, set off as a stage effect to mark the king's entrance onstage in a scene at Cardinal Wolsey's palace. The entire Globe was destroyed within the hour.

In June 1614 it had been rebuilt, this time with a tiled gallery roof. It was pulled down in 1644, two years after the Puritans closed all theatres, to make way for tenement dwellings.

See Globe Theatre in volume 5 of the Micropaedia.

Why do some animals glow in the dark?

Bioluminescence or "living light" is found in fishes and insects, as well as bacteria, fungi, and marine invertebrae. It is due to a chemical reaction and is virtually 100 percent efficient; i.e., very little heat is given off in the process.

Light production appears to be associated with the survival and protection of a species. Many deep-sea fishes dangle luminous lures to attract food or show light organs that disguise their form from enemies, frighten predators or simply light the way in the darkness of the ocean depths.

The firefly uses its light as a mating signal. The male flashes spontaneously in flight, while the female watches from the ground. Upon seeing a flash, the female flashes a response after an interval of about 2 seconds. It is this which attracts the male. Males flash on average every $5\frac{1}{2}$ seconds, so this interval between male signal and female response is crucial to successful recognition and mating.

See BIOLUMINESCENCE in volume 2 of the Micropaedia.

What happened to the gold standard?

The early 20th century was the great era of the international gold standard. Gold coins circulated in most of the world; paper money, whether issued by private banks or by government, was convertible on demand into gold coins or gold bullion at an official price; and bank deposits were convertible into either gold coin or paper currency that was itself convertible into gold. There was, in effect, a single world money called by different names in different countries.

Its great advantage was that – if permitted to operate – it greatly limits the power of any national government and prevents it from engaging in irresponsible monetary expansion. This was also its great disadvantage. In an era of big government and of full employment policies, a real gold standard would tie the hands of national governments in one of the most important areas of policy.

World War I ended the real international gold standard. Though restored after the war, it was a far cry from the prewar gold standard. If the Great Depression had not occurred, this system might have matured and improved. But the Depression brought the managed gold standards to a quick end. Britain, in 1931, became the first major country to leave the gold standard.

See MONEY in volume 24 of the Macropaedia.

Where does all the world's gold go?

Jewelry remains the largest single use for gold in all parts of the world. Most gold used in jewelry is alloyed with silver, copper, and a little zinc to produce various shades of yellow gold, or with nickel, copper, and zinc to produce white gold.

In the electrical and electronics industries, gold is applied as a finish to electrical connectors, and as a thin coating over palladium in telephone relay contacts. It is also used in the manufacture of transistors and microelectronic assemblies, and to protect etched circuit boards in storage.

Dental applications include wrought and cast gold alloys with a gold content of 60 percent or more along with silver, copper, and sometimes platinum; the rest of the alloy consists of palladium.

Small amounts of gold are used in decorating china and glassware and to provide heat-reflecting surfaces for window glass. Some gold goes into heat-reflecting shields in aircraft, and small quantities find applications in the medical and chemical fields.

Monetary use of gold is rare.

See EXTRACTION AND PROCESSING INDUSTRIES in volume 21 of the Macropaedia.

Did golf originate in Scotland?

The origin of golf has long been a subject of controversy. Broadly, the issue has been whether its birthplace is Scotland or Holland.

Its antiquity in Scotland is beyond question, though its exact roots have never been traced. The Scottish claim has at any rate documentary proof of its long lineage; in the first written reference, the Parliament of King James II of 1457 decreed that both "Fute-ball and Golfe be utterly cryed downe" because they interfered with the practice of archery, which was necessary for the defense of the realm. So it seems that golf had become a popular obsession in Scotland before the middle of the 15th century.

One of the continental games which bears some resemblance to golf is *chole* (*choulla* or *choulle*). It was a cross-country pastime in which each side, whether one player or several, used one ball and played to a prearranged target. After each three-stroke turn the opposing player (or side) had the right to hit the ball into any available hazard, the more difficult the better. Such interference with the play of an opponent is, of course, utterly alien to golf.

Comparisons between ancient continental games and Scottish golf result in the balance of evidence in favour of Scotland as the country of origin.

See SPORTS in volume 28 of the Macropaedia.

Is Pidgin English a language without grammar?

Pidgin languages spring from the initial, non-intimate contacts between speakers of different languages, when quick comprehension is more highly valued than grammatical correctness or fine shades of meaning. Grammatical categories such as number, tense, and voice are almost absent from pidgin, as they are from many languages, but pidgin is not devoid of grammar: Melanesian pidgin, for example, inflects its pronouns, adjectives, and verbs.

Since vocabulary is restricted (to about 2,000 words in Melanesian pidgin), each word has a large range of meaning. For many concepts, phrases are used rather than single words; thus *skru bilong arm* means elbow, *haus pepa*, "house for paper", means office and *haus kuk*, "house for cooking", means kitchen.

See LANGUAGES OF THE WORLD in volume 22 of the Macropaedia.

What is the "greenhouse effect"?

The global concentration of carbon dioxide has been steadily increasing since the mid-1800s, mainly as a result of the burning of such fossil fuels as coal and oil. Through the mechanism known as the greenhouse effect, carbon dioxide in the atmosphere absorbs thermal infrared radiation emitted by the surface of the Earth and reradiates a portion of it back toward the Earth. Thus, as the amount of atmospheric carbon dioxide increases, the average temperature of the Earth's surface also increases.

See CLIMATE AND WEATHER in volume 16 of the Macropaedia.

How have musicians' concepts of harmony changed?

Central to the idea of harmony throughout the history of Western music are the ideas of consonance and dissonance. A consonant chord is perceived as being at rest, whereas a dissonant one is in a state of tension that requires resolution. The relative degree of tension in a chord is not intrinsic: the presence of consonance and dissonance are associated with particular chords and intervals according to their place in the context of the prevailing style. Broadly speaking, the group of chords considered consonant has expanded constantly throughout musical history. It was not until the 15th century that thirds and sixths were heard as consonant, and seconds and sevenths retained their dissonant associations until the work of Debussy and Schoenberg, among others, in the late 19th and early 20th centuries, gave them a place among the consonant chords.

See HARMONY in volume 5 of the Micropaedia.

Did Abelard and Héloïse meet again?

Early in the 12th century, the teacher Peter Abelard was given as a pupil the young Héloïse, niece of one of the clergy of the cathedral of Paris, Canon Fulbert. Abelard and Héloïse fell in love, had a son they named Astralabe, and married secretly. To escape her uncle's wrath, Héloïse withdrew into the convent of Argenteuil outside Paris. Abelard suffered castration at Fulbert's instigation. He entered the royal abbey of Saint-Denis near Paris and made Héloïse become a nun at Argenteuil.

Years later, Héloïse had become the head of a new foundation of nuns called the Paraclete. Abelard became abbot of the community and provided it with a justification of the nun's way of life; in this he emphasized the virtue of literary study. He also provided books of hymns he had composed, and he and Héloïse made a collection of their own love letters and religious correspondence.

Abelard's body lies alongside that of Héloïse in the cemetery of Père-Lachaise in Paris.

See ABELARD, PETER in volume 1 of the Micropaedia.

What is the Hippocratic oath?

Perhaps the greatest legacy of Hippocrates (born around 460 BC) was the charter of medical conduct known as the oath of Hippocrates, which has been adopted as a pattern by medical men throughout the ages and is still used during the ceremony of graduation at many universities and schools of medicine:

"I will look upon him who shall have taught me this Art even as one of my parents. I will share my substance with him, and I will supply his necessities, if he be in need. I will regard his offspring even as my own brethren, and I will teach them this Art, if they would learn it, without fee or covenant. I will impart this Art by precept, by lecture and by every mode of teaching, not only to my own sons but to the sons of him who has taught me, and to disciples bound by covenant and oath, according to the Law of Medicine.

"The regimen I adopt shall be for the benefit of my patients according to my ability and judgment, and not for their hurt or for any wrong. I will give no deadly drug to any, though it be asked of me, nor will I counsel such, and especially I will not aid a woman to procure abortion. Whatsoever house I enter, there will I go for the benefit of the sick, refraining from all wrongdoing or corruption, and especially from any act of seduction, of male or female, of bond or free. Whatsoever things I see or hear concerning the life of men, in my attendance on the sick or even apart therefrom, which ought not to be noised abroad, I will keep silence thereon, counting such things to be as sacred secrets."

See MEDICINE in volume 23 of the Macropaedia.

Was Homer a woman?

By Homer is meant the poet or poets primarily responsible for the *Iliad* and *Odyssey*, the two great epic poems of ancient Greece. Little is known of him beyond the fact that his was the name attached by the Greeks themselves to the two great poems.

The dearth of objective information about him has led to such theories as that of a German critic and philologist that the epics were in origin a kind of spontaneous emanation from the whole people, or Samuel Butler (1835–1902) that the *Odyssey* was composed by a woman.

The absence of hard facts about Homer puzzled but did not deter the ancient Greeks. They developed fantastic pseudobiographies about him. The longest to have survived purports to be by Herodotus himself, and does not scruple to assign to Homer several generations of ancestors and a detailed catalog of travels: the work is quite devoid of objective truth.

Modern scholars conclude that there *was* a major poet called Homer, that he was an Ionian, that he was substantially the composer of the *Iliad*, and that, whether or not it was directly his work, he was at the very least the inspirer of the *Odyssey*. Anything else is conjecture.

See THE HOMERIC EPICS in volume 20 of the Macropaedia.

Is it wise to eat a honeycomb sandwich?

In the production of components that must bear high loads yet be as light as possible, aerospace fabricators have evolved a technique for changing the properties of a material by engineering.

The most notable example is the honeycomb sandwich. The core of the sandwich is the honeycomb, a structure composed of row upon row of framed cells, or holes. To each side of the core are bonded extremely thin sheets of metal. The sandwich is far lighter yet has greater resistance to bending than a comparable thickness of metal plate.

See MANUFACTURING INDUSTRIES in volume 21 of the Macropaedia.

Who first explained how we see?

In a book published in 1604, Johannes Kepler made an analysis of the process of vision that provided the foundation for all the advances in the understanding and structure of the human eye. Kepler wrote that every point on a luminous body in the field of vision emits rays of light in all directions, but that only those rays can enter the eye that impinge on the pupil. All of these rays are then refracted to meet again at a single point on the retina, identified by Kepler as the sensitive receptor of the eye.

If the eye is not normal, the rays come to a point not on the retina but in front of it or behind it. In either case blurred vision is the result. For over three centuries eyeglasses had helped older people to see better. But nobody before Kepler was able to explain how these little pieces of curved glass had worked.

See the biography of KEPLER in volume 22 of the Macropaedia.

What is the "I Ching"?

I Ching means "Classic of Changes", and is one of the Five Classics of Confucianism. It has long fascinated Chinese and Westerners alike. Though the book was originally used for divination, its influence on Chinese minds and its universal popularity is due to a system of cosmology that involves man and nature in a single system. The uniqueness of the *I Ching* consists in its presentation of 64 symbolic hexagrams, that, if properly understood and interpreted, are said to contain profound meanings applicable to daily life. Throughout the ages, *I Ching* enthusiasts have claimed that the book is a means of understanding, and even controlling, future events. The text of the *I Ching* is often expressed in cryptic, thought-provoking language, and so allows the user considerable leeway in interpreting its significance for him or her.

See I CHING in volume 6 of the Micropaedia.

What is the difference between infection and infectious disease?

In human beings, an infectious disease is a process caused by an organism, most commonly a microorganism, that impairs a person's health. An infection, in contrast, is the invasion of the body by organisms and the reactions of tissues to their presence or to the toxins that they produce, whether or not health is affected. Thus, a person may be infected but not have an infectious disease. This principle is illustrated by the use of vaccines for the prevention of infectious diseases: a virus such as that which causes measles may be partially inactivated and used as an immunizing agent; this produces a measles infection in the recipient but generally causes no discernible alteration in the state of health. It produces immunity to measles without producing the infectious disease.

See INFECTIOUS DISEASES in volume 21 of the Macropaedia.

Do insects use antifreeze?

In cool weather, insects must remain in the sun to warm themselves. Many butterflies must spread their wings to collect heat before they can fly. A moth raises its temperature by vibrating its wings or "shivering" before taking flight. The heat generated in this way is conserved by hairs or scales that maintain a layer of insulating air around the body.

For more extreme conditions, a few insects tolerate ice formation in their body fluids; for most, however, survival of the winter in cold latitudes means resistance to freezing. This resistance results partly from accumulation of large quantities of glycerol as an antifreeze, and partly from physical changes that permit super-

cooling of the blood to temperatures far below freezing point.

Insects are adapted to every land and freshwater habitat where food is available, from deserts and jungles to glacial fields, from cold mountain streams to stagnant lowland ponds, brackish streams and hot springs. There are even fly larvae that can live in pools of crude petroleum, eating other insects that fall in.

See INSECTS in volume 21 of the Macropaedia.

Is intelligence hereditary?

In the 19th century, Sir Francis Galton analyzed a large number of pedigrees of distinguished statesmen, scientists, military commanders, literary men, artists, divines, and other groups. He concluded that high intelligence (as manifest in such activities) strongly depends on heredity. Galton accorded environmental influences little importance.

Subsequent studies strongly tend to endorse Galton's conclusions that intelligence runs in families. Except in such extreme cases as infantile malnutrition, environment indeed seems to play a minor role; for example, adopted children resemble their biological parents in measured intelligence more than they do their foster parents. Monozygotic ("identical") twins reared apart still tend to be more similar in intelligence than are dizygotic twins raised in the same home.

Specific aspects of intelligence behaviour (verbal ability, spatial intelligence, and word fluency) have strong genetic dependence, too. In one especially sophisticated study, numerical ability also was found to be significantly heritable.

See INNATE FACTORS IN HUMAN BEHAVIOUR in volume 14 of the Macropaedia.

Who spent $300,000 to prove the worth of his invention?

Edwin H. Armstrong, born in New York City in 1890, laid the foundation for much of modern radio and electronic circuitry, including the regenerative and superheterodyne circuits and the FM system.

At the age of 14, fired by reading of the exploits of Guglielmo Marconi in sending the first wireless message across the Atlantic, Armstrong decided to become an inventor. He built a maze of wireless apparatus in the family attic, and began the solitary, secretive work that absorbed his life. Wireless was then in the stage of crude spark-gap transmitters and iron-filing receivers, and Armstrong joined in the hunt for improved instruments.

In 1933 he secured four patents on advanced circuits that were to solve the problem of eliminating static from radio. Instead of varying the amplitude or power of radio waves to carry voice or music, as in all radio before then, the new system varied or modulated the waves' frequency (number of waves per second) over a wide band of frequencies. As a result, FM radio, as it later became known, (FM for frequency modulation) made possible the first clear, high-fidelity broadcasting.

Since the new system required a basic change in transmitters and receivers, it was not embraced with any alacrity by the established radio industry. Armstrong had to build the first full-scale FM station himself in 1939 at a cost of over $300,000 to prove its worth. When FM slowly established itself, Armstrong found himself entrapped in an interminable patent suit to retain his invention. Ill and ageing in 1954, with most of his wealth gone in the battle for FM, he took his own life.

FM is now the preferred system in radio, the required sound channel in all television, and the dominant medium in mobile radio, microwave relay, and space-satellite communications.

See the biography of ARMSTRONG in volume 1 of the Micropaedia.

Why Istanbul not Constantinople?

Istanbul is the largest city and seaport of Turkey and formerly the capital of the Byzantine and Ottoman empires. For 2,500 years it has stood between conflicting surges of religion, culture, and imperial power.

According to legend, the leader of the Greeks who built the city about 657 BC was called Byzas – hence its ancient name of Byzantium. In AD 196 the Roman Emperor Septimius Severus, having razed the town for opposing him in a civil war, rebuilt it and named it Augusta Antonina in honour of his son. In AD 330 when Constantine the Great dedicated the city as his capital, he called it New Rome. The coinage, nevertheless, continued to be stamped Byzantium until he ordered the substitution of Constantinopolis.

In the 13th century Arabs used the word "Istinpolin", a "name" they heard Byzantines use – *eis ten polin* – which was actually Greek for "in the city". Over the centuries, through a series of speech permutations, this name became Istanbul – a change made official by Turkey in 1926.

See ISTANBUL in volume 22 of the Macropaedia.

Was Ivan so Terrible?

Ivan IV was proclaimed grand prince of Moscow on his father's death in 1533, when Ivan himself was only three years old. He was later the first formally proclaimed tsar of Russia. The child's mother ruled in his name until her death, allegedly by poison, in 1538. Ivan never accused anyone of this crime, although her favourite was thrown into prison, and his sister, who had been Ivan's nurse, was forced to become a nun.

Ivan's first independent action took place at the age of 13, when he ordered the seizure in his presence of the leader of one of the court factions; at 15, he ordered a nobleman's tongue to be cut out "for uttering rude words."

Many of the tsar's acts shocked his contemporaries, particularly the brutality of his public executions; his methods of disposing of those churchmen who displeased him were extremely cruel, as was his decimation of the city of Novgorod the Great. But in the context of his

day, his methods were perhaps not more extreme than those employed elsewhere.

Ivan was undoubtedly a passionate man, and as he did not sanction extramarital relationships for a ruler, his wives were changed with great frequency. He had six wives (a seventh union not being recognised by the Church); of these, three died, one survived him, and two were divorced and forced to enter nunneries. Ivan also discussed with the English ambassador the possibility of marrying one of Queen Elizabeth's ladies-in-waiting, Mary Hastings; he had been anxious to cement relationships with England since 1553, and in 1556 he even toyed with the idea of abdicating and living in England. But he remained on the Russian throne until his death in 1584.

See IVAN IV in volume 6 of the Micropaedia.

Who arranges the flowers in Japan?

Until 1868 Japanese flower arrangement was generally a man's avocation, engaged in primarily by Buddhist priests, warriors, and the nobility. Following the Meiji restoration and particularly after the beginning of the 20th century, it was taken up by large numbers of women. Men, however, still head most of the principal schools.

The total number of schools throughout Japan in the 20th century is believed to number from 2,000 to 3,000, varying in size from several thousand to millions of adherents. Each school has its own rules of arrangement, though styles may differ only slightly from one another. All arrangements are asymmetrical and achieve a three-dimensional effect. The traditional styles are still taught, many with modern variations, but the bolder, less restrained, and unconventional free-style forms of arrangement now seem to be the most popular.

Japanese flower arranging has influenced that of the West considerably, particularly in the mid-20th century.

See DECORATIVE ARTS AND FURNISHINGS in volume 17 of the Macropaedia.

How impenetrable is the jungle?

In modern usage, jungle has come to mean tropical forest, with an idea of luxuriant, tangled, inpenetrable vegetation in a hot, steamy environment, teeming with wildlife.

The rain forest takes a wide variety of forms but very seldom approaches its popular image; in fact, it is darkly shaded, with little ground cover, and is fairly easy to travel in. Where light can penetrate to the ground, however, as along tracks and riverbanks, a dense and tangled mass of vegetation appears, and because most people see the forest from a track or from a boat it is easy to believe in the impenetrable jungle.

See ECOSYSTEMS in volume 17 of the Macropaedia.

What is the doctrine of karman?

Rarely disputed and thus generally accepted by Hindus are the doctrine of transmigration and rebirth and its complement, the belief in *karman* – that previous acts determine the condition into which a being, after a stay in heaven or hell, is reborn. The *karman*, acting like a clockwork that, while running down, always winds itself up, binds the selves of beings to the world, compelling them to go, in unremitting restlessness, through an endless series of births and deaths.

This belief is connected with the traditional Indian view of society and earthly life. It has given rise to an acquiescence that may verge upon fatalism – the belief that any misfortune is the effect of *karman*, of one's deeds, and so one's own doing – and to the conviction that the course of world history is conditioned by the collective *karman*.

Such doctrines also encourage the view that mundane life is not true existence and that human endeavour ought to be directed toward a permanent interruption of the mechanism of *karman* and transmigration – that is, toward escaping forever from the impermanence that is an inescapable feature of mundane existence.

See HINDUISM in volume 20 of the Macropaedia.

What is the quickest way of learning a new skill?

Learning a new skill is accomplished most quickly and perfection is achieved most rapidly if the skill is practised in the manner that most closely approximates the final performance. "Walking through" a movement is a good way to be introduced to a new skill, such as a dance step. As soon as possible, the tempo should be advanced to the proper rate. Every element – tempo, stride, force – should match in practice that of the hoped-for performance.

This is because training is specific to the point that slow running does not improve sprinting; badminton play does not enhance tennis ability. Each pattern of movement has its own characteristic postures, interplays between opposing muscles, and sequences in which motion is started, stopped, speeded, and slowed. Through training these patterns are imprinted in the nervous system and are "replayed" automatically on signal, as when the music begins or the starting pistol is fired.

See EXERCISE AND PHYSICAL CONDITIONING in volume 19 of the Macropaedia.

How was a Roman legion organized?

Roman military might rose as the empire of Alexander, built on superior military tactics, was crumbling in the hands of his former generals. The Romans learned by defeat that the simple phalanx of infantry, a "human wall", is not suited to rough ground.

They evolved a new fighting unit – the legion. A typical legion in the time of the republic was drawn up in three lines. The first two lines consisted of ten maniples (1 maniple = 120 men in 10 ranks of 12). In the third line light infantry were alternated with reserves and cavalry. From front to rear, one maniple from each line formed a cohort, numbering 420 men.

The two famous Roman infantry weapons were the *pilum*, or javelin, and the *gladius*, a cut-and-thrust sword. Aggression was the Roman's best defense. The first line made a running attack, hurling javelins and diving in with swords before the enemy had time to recover. Then came the second line. Only a resolute foe could rally from the two successive shocks.

See THE THEORY AND CONDUCT OF WAR in volume 29 of the Macropaedia.

Where did the first key turn in a lock?

The lock – for securing a door or receptacle – originated in the Near East. The oldest known example was found in the ruins of the palace of Khorsabad near Nineveh. Possibly 4,000 years old, it is of the type known as a pin-tumbler. The key is a large wooden bar, something like a toothbrush in shape.

The Romans were the first to make small keys for locks – some so small that they could be worn on the fingers as rings. They also invented the padlock, which is found throughout the Near and Far East, where it was probably independently invented by the Chinese.

In the Middle Ages, great skill and a high degree of workmanship were employed in making metal locks, especially by the German metalworkers of Nürnberg. The moving parts of the locks were closely fitted and finished, and the exteriors were lavishly decorated. Even the keys were often virtual works of art.

The lock industry was in its heyday in the mid-19th century. With the rapidly expanding economy that followed the Industrial Revolution, the demand for locks grew tremendously.

See LOCK in volume 7 of the Micropaedia.

Did Old London Bridge fall down?

In 1176 Peter of Colechurch undertook the building of the first stone bridge with masonry foundations to be built in a swiftly flowing river having a large tidal range. His London Bridge was to consist of 19 pointed arches, each with about a 7-metre span, built on piers 6 metres wide. The 13th arch from the city was designed as a tollgate for merchant shipping with a military drawbridge.

The foundations were built inside cofferdams made by driving timber sheathing piles, which held the pier stones in place. Obstructions encountered in pile driving resulted in the span of the arches varying from 5 to 10 metres. At the base of the piers there were protective "starlings" made of loose stone filling enclosed by piles, so that the waterway was reduced to a quarter of its original width and the tide flowed under the narrow archways like a millrace.

The bridge, nevertheless, was completed in 1209 and survived, together with its famous tunnel-like street of shops and houses, for more than 600 years.

See PUBLIC WORKS in volume 26 of the Macropaedia.

Why is magic mysterious?

Magic forms the core of many religious systems and plays a central social role in many nonliterate cultures.

There are usually considered to be three main elements in magic: the spell or incantation, the rite itself, and the ritual condition of the performer. Excellent examples of spells are recorded from the earliest times, especially in Greco-Egyptian papyruses of the 1st to the 4th century AD. The frequently archaic and esoteric vocabulary of spells may represent in a symbolic sense the mysterious nature of spiritual power and in a practical sense the restriction of human access to it. Personal names are commonly used in spells by magicians to work good or harm upon individuals. This power is regarded as so strong in some societies that each individual has two names – a "real" one that is kept a careful secret, and an everyday title, through which no magic can be worked. Gods and spirits are commonly believed to have special magic names, known only to a chosen few.

Even in societies where magic is regarded as an everyday and "natural" phenomenon, it is nevertheless considered as potentially dangerous and polluting, as is any sacred or religious object or activity. Both the magician and the rite itself will be surrounded by taboos, purification ceremonies and the like, and failure to observe these precautions nullifies the magic.

See MAGIC in volume 7 of the Micropaedia.

Did mapping come before writing?

Babylonians drew maps on clay tablets, of which the oldest specimens found so far have been dated about 2300 BC. It may be assumed that map making goes back much further and that it began among nonliterate peoples.

There are numerous examples of not yet literate peoples showing surprising aptitudes in depicting essential features of their localities and travels. During Captain Charles Wilkes's exploration of the South Seas in the 1840s, a friendly islander drew a good sketch of the whole Tuamoto Archipelago on the deck of the captain's bridge. In North America the Pawnee Indians were reputed to have used star charts painted on elk skin to guide them on night marches across the plains. Montezuma is said to have given Cortés a map of the whole Mexican gulf area painted on cloth, while Pedro de Gamboa reported that the Incas used sketch maps and cut some in stone to show relief features. Many specimens of early Eskimo sketch maps on skin, wood, and bone have been found.

See MAPPING AND SURVEYING in volume 23 of the Macropaedia.

Are there canals on Mars?

The so-called canals of Mars are apparent systems of rectilinear markings on the surface of the planet, that are now known to be illusions caused by the chance alignment of large craters and other features. They were the subject of much controversy in the late 19th and early 20th centuries. The American astronomer Percival Lowell became the leader of those who believed the markings to be bands of vegetation, kilometres wide, bordering irrigation ditches dug by intelligent beings to carry water from the polar caps. Lowell and others described networks, studded with dark intersections called oases and covering much of the surface of the planet; most astronomers could see no canals and many doubted their reality.

The controversy was finally resolved only when pictures were made from several hundred kilometres above the surface of Mars by the Mariner 6 and 7 spacecraft in 1969. These showed nothing resembling a network of channels.

See MARS, CANALS OF in volume 7 of the Micropaedia.

How did Matisse bring about a revolution in art?

Henri Matisse displayed little interest in art until he was 20. When he became a professional artist in 1891, he was far from being a typical Left

Bank bohemian art student: the 19th-century gospel of work derived from a middle class, northern French upbringing, was to mark his entire career, and was soon accompanied by a thoroughly bourgeois appearance which was odd for a leading member of the Parisian avant-garde.

At first a provincial with tastes that were old-fashioned in a Paris already familiar with the Post-Impressionism of Cézanne, Gauguin, and van Gogh, Matisse became a familiar figure in the circles where modern art was being produced and discussed.

He spent the summer of 1905 on the Mediterranean, where in the dazzling sunshine his theoretically realistic colours exploded into an emotional display of complementaries. Matisse quickly became the leader of Fauvism (from *les fauves* – "the wild beasts"), the first of the important "isms" of 20th-century painting.

See MATISSE in volume 7 of the Micropaedia.

How was metal first discovered?

It is generally agreed that the first metals known to man were gold, silver, and copper, which occurred in the native or metallic state. Such native metals became known and were appreciated for their ornamental and utilitarian values during the latter part of the Stone Age.

An essential step towards the Metal Age was the discovery that metals could be melted and cast to shape in molds.

Man needed a stronger metal than native copper. Possibly more by accident than intent, he discovered that certain copper ores containing the tin-bearing material cassiterite could be treated in a charcoal fire at a red heat to produce an alloy of copper and tin known as bronze. Bronze is harder than copper, has a lower melting temperature, and casts more readily, producing sounder castings.

During the Bronze Age the Egyptians introduced the lost-wax process. In this method, an exact model or pattern of the object to be cast is made in wax, then covered with clay to form the mold. The composite is heated to harden the mold and to melt the wax, which drains off, leaving an exact negative impression. This is filled with molten metal and allowed to solidify.

By 1400 BC, iron was assuming increasing importance. Iron does not exist on Earth except in ores, but meteoric iron, while rare, has been known from a very early date. The earliest record of iron smelting dates from about 1300 BC. By 1200 BC, iron had attained sufficient importance for this date to be used as marking the beginning of the Iron Age.

See EXTRACTION AND PROCESSING INDUSTRIES in volume 21 of the Macropaedia.

What part do carbon granules play in a microphone?

The first successful instrument for converting acoustic power into electric power was the electromagnetic telephone transmitter used by Alexander Graham Bell in 1876. The term microphone was first used in 1878. By virtue of the variable resistance of a loose contact, the loose granules of carbon in a carbon telephone transmitter, under the influence of varying sound pressure, introduce a variable resistance into the circuit. This controls the energy delivered by a battery. As a result, the sound waves are converted into corresponding but amplified variations in electric current.

See SOUND in volume 27 of the Macropaedia.

What causes migraine?

The underlying cause of migraine is unknown. At one time or another, various investigators have attempted to link migraine to allergy, epilepsy, or other conditions, but the evidence has been unconvincing. Several studies have suggested an abnormality in the regulation of serotonin, a chemical involved in transmitting impulses to the brain. The observed chemical changes in patients with migraine, however, have not always been consistent.

Treatment consists of using vasoconstrictor and analgesic drugs during the attacks and psychological guidance for the patient between attacks. Persons with migraine are characteristically perfectionistic, self-demanding, hard-working and inflexible. They commonly set impossibly high standards for themselves and, less often, for others. When affected persons come to understand these feelings and realize the fatigue and resentment they engender in themselves, they are often able to establish more realistic ways of approaching life. Headaches tend to decline in frequency at the same time.

See HEADACHE in volume 5 of the Micropaedia.

Are there tides on the Moon?

Just as the Moon raises tides on the Earth, the Earth, with its far greater mass, raises tides on the Moon. Because there is no surface water on the Moon, it is only necessary to consider the tides in the solid material; that is, the bodily tides.

Evidence suggests that two types of phenomena on the Moon are tidally related. Temporary changes in the appearance of small areas occasionally have been noted. The sighting of glows of light, colour changes, and obscuration of detail in such areas have been reported since the late 18th century, and similar observations were made even before the invention of the telescope. These lunar transient events seem to occur unpredictably, but statistically they are observed more frequently at perigee (at the point in the Moon's orbit when it is closest to the Earth), when the overall tidal effect of the Earth on the Moon is greatest. They may represent the appearance of small quantities of gas and dust, tidally released through cracks in the Moon's surface.

Seismic signals, which measure interior disturbances in the Moon, also provide evidence. One type of signal occurred at each perigee and was found to originate at very nearly the same place each time. Because it was extremely unlikely that meteorites would fall precisely at each perigee in the same place, it was concluded that the disturbances causing the signals were moonquakes, triggered by extreme tidal conditions. A second group of signals were believed to be tidally related because they were found to occur sometimes at perigee and also at apogee (when the Moon is furthest from the Earth).

See MECHANICS in volume 23 of the Macropaedia.

What did Mozart think of Beethoven?

Ludwig van Beethoven is generally regarded as the greatest composer who ever lived. His father was a musician, but declined into alcoholism, with the result that the Beethoven family became steadily poorer. By the age of 11 Beethoven had to leave school. His father, observing in him signs of a talent for the piano, tried to make his son a child prodigy like Mozart but without success. It was not until his adolescence that Beethoven, on his own account, began to attract mild attention.

By 1787 he had made such progress that he was sent to Vienna to study with Mozart. The visit was cut short when, after only two months, Beethoven received the news of his mother's death. According to tradition, Mozart was highly impressed by Beethoven's powers of improvisation and told some friends that "this young man will make a great name for himself in the world".

See the biography of BEETHOVEN in volume 14 of the Macropaedia.

Who is most likely to commit murder?

The majority of homicides are committed within the family or between close friends. About half occur as the result of trivial altercation In the United States, the method is equally distributed among gunning, stabbing, and beatings. In contrast, guns are rarely used in England: assailants often use blunt objects that happen to be on hand at the time.

The age of homicide offenders in America is predominantly 20 to 24, but in England it is a little higher, though both countries report an increasing use of violence by youthful offenders. Many early studies have reported that participants in homicide in the United States do not generally have previous records, but one thorough study reported that nearly two-thirds of the offenders had prior arrest records. In England, more than one-half of convicted violent offenders have had previous records of arrest for non-violent offenses; and 20 percent have had previous convictions for crimes of violence.

Of all crimes, homicide has the highest "clearance rate" (that is, more murders are solved than any other crime); the rate is around 90 percent in most countries for which statistics are available. The conviction rate, however, appears to be somewhat lower.

See Crime and Punishment in volume 16 of the Macropaedia.

How fast do nails grow?

In the primates (including man) the fingers and toes end in nails rather than in claws. Nails are similar to hair in composition (keratin), but, unlike hair, nails grow continuously, with no normal periods of rest. If they were protected from wear, they would extend to prodigious lengths, growing in a twisted fashion like ram's horns.

Nails grow at the rate of about 0·1 mm per day (roughly one-third more slowly than hair). Growth is slower in winter than in summer, and slower in infants and old people than in vigorous young adults. It requires about three months for a whole nail to replace itself and habitual nail biting actually speeds up growth.

See Integumentary Systems in volume 21 of the Macropaedia.

Why give a child a "bad" name?

One of the most important elements of the naming process concerns the meaning and association of the names. To get a "meaning" of a name like Philip, one must go back to its original Greek version, Philippos, which means "lover of horses". This meaning of names frequently gets lost, however.

Names that have no "meaning" (above all not for the person who chooses the name) still can have associations. Although "Mary" and "John" have no specific "meaning", they were the names of important persons in the Christian religion and therefore have been used very frequently. An association may be so strong that it overwhelms the "meaning" of a name, even a disagreeable meaning; *e.g.*, the association with the cult of St. Demetrios made the name Demetrios one of the most popular in the Greek Orthodox Church, though its meaning is "belonging to (the pagan goddess) Demeter."

In the majority of cases, children are given "good", likable, and propitious names. However, in some cultures (*e.g.*, in some parts of sub-Saharan Africa, formerly in China, and sporadically in ancient Greece), the children are (or were) sometimes given "bad" names with meanings like "ugly", "disagreeable", or "crippled". The purpose of such names is to make the child undesirable to demons.

See Names in volume 24 of the Macropaedia.

Did Nero fiddle while Rome burned?

The emperor Nero was brought up by his mother Agrippina, the sister of Caligula, who after poisoning her second husband, incestuously became the wife of her uncle, the emperor Claudius. Ceaselessly pursuing her intrigues to bring Nero to power, she eliminated her opponents, and probably poisoned Claudius himself.

Nero was entirely under the influence of his terrifying mother, but up to the fifth year of his reign his biographers cite only acts of generosity on his account. His nocturnal rioting in the streets was a scandal as early as 56 AD (the second year of his reign), but the emergence of real brutality can be seen in his putting to death his mother and his wife in 59 and 62. He gave reign to inordinate artistic pretensions, and was drawn to preachers of novel cults, perhaps even to St. Paul.

Taking advantage of the fire that ravaged Rome in 64, he had the city reconstructed in the Greek style and built a prodigious palace which, had it been finished, would have covered a third of Rome. During the fire Nero was at his villa at Antium 56 kilometres from Rome and cannot be held responsible. Nor, despite the additions made centuries later to histories and biographies, should he be charged with the first persecutions of the Christians, because there were then so few Christians in Rome.

See NERO in volume 8 of the Micropaedia.

When was the news told in verse?

Before the advent of the newspaper, the rhymed accounts of current events in the form of ballads were the chief source of spectacular news. Every sensational public happening was immediately clapped into rhyme. These ballads were a lively commodity, providing employment for a troop of hack poets.

The ballads were printed on broadsheets, about the size of handbills. A crude woodcut often headed the sheet, and under the title it was specified that the ballad was to be sung to the tune of some popular air. Musical notation seldom appeared on the broadsides; those who sold them in the streets and at country fairs sang their wares so that anyone unfamiliar with the tune could learn it by listening a few times to the balladmonger's rendition.

Few of the topical pieces long survived the events which gave them birth, but a good number of pathetic tragedies, such as "The Children in the Wood" and broadsides about Robin Hood, Guy of Warwick, and other national heroes, remained perennial favourites.

See THE ART OF LITERATURE in volume 23 of the Macropaedia.

What laws did Newton define for motion and gravity?

Newton's first two laws of motion were anticipated by Galileo, whose observations uncovered the fact that bodies maintain uniform motion, (or are at rest) when no force is acting on them.

Newton's three laws of motion are concerned with the effect of force on motion. They are:

(1) every body continues in its state of rest, or of uniform motion in a straight line, unless compelled by a force to change that state;

(2) the rate of change of momentum (velocity × mass) is proportional to and along the line of the force;

(3) to every action corresponds an equal and opposite reaction.

Newton's law of universal gravitation states that two bodies attract each other with a force that is along the line connecting the bodies, is proportional to the product of the masses of the bodies, and is inversely proportional to the square of the distance between the bodies. The law is universal since it is applicable to the motion of a planet around the Sun as well as to the falling of a stone (or apple).

See MECHANICS in volume 23 of the Macropaedia.

Where is the source of the Nile?

The Nile, the father of African rivers, flows northward through Africa into the Mediterranean. Its name comes from the Greek Neilos, but the ancient Egyptians called the river Ar or Aur ("black") in allusion to the colour of the sediments carried by the river when it is in flood. Nile mud is black enough to have given the land itself its oldest name, Kem or Kemi, which also means "black".

The Egyptians were probably familiar with the Nile as far as Khartoum, but did not know its source. The river was associated with the worship of the god Apis or Hapi, the bull of Memphis, since it provided them with water with which to irrigate their crops. Greek geographers explored the river to the first cataract – there are six cataracts caused by outcropping crystalline rocks crossing the river's course and hindering navigation.

The Nile is formed of three principal streams, the Blue Nile and the Atbara, which flow from the Highlands of Ethiopia, and the White Nile, the headstreams of which flow into lakes Victoria and Albert. The farthest headstream may be regarded as the Kagera River, which rises in the highlands of Burundi. The Nile proper, however, rises from Lake Victoria.

The search for the source of the Nile led several European and Turkish explorers to venture southwards from Egypt – notably Burton, Speke, and Baker. Their discoveries, though the subject of much argument at the time, are now commonly held to have settled the origin and course of the Nile.

See AFRICA in volume 13 of the Macropaedia.

What causes the northern lights?

The auroras are luminous phenomena of the upper atmosphere that occur in the high latitudes of both hemispheres; auroras in the Northern Hemisphere are called Aurora Borealis, or northern lights; in the Southern Hemisphere, Aurora Australis, or southern lights.

Auroras are caused by the interaction of energetic particles from outside the atmosphere with atoms of the upper atmosphere. This occurs in zones about 2,000 kilometres in diameter around the geomagnetic poles; during periods of great solar activity the Aurora Borealis has been seen as far south as Mexico.

The lights take many forms, including curtains, arcs, rays, bands, and fan-shaped coronas. The uniform arc is the most stable form and sometimes persists for hours.

See AURORA in volume 1 of the Micropaedia.

Which is the world's largest ocean?

The Pacific occupies about a third of the Earth's surface and is by far the largest of the three oceans that extend northwards from Antarctica. It has double the area and more than double the water of the Atlantic. At 166 million square kilometres, the Pacific's area exceeds that of the whole land surface of the globe, Antarctica included, with Africa counted twice. From north to south it stretches for 15,500 kilometres, through 135° of latitude. It also contains the greatest known ocean deep, the Mariana Trench (11,034 metres).

See OCEANS in volume 25 of the Macropaedia.

What form did the first Olympic Games take?

It is reasonably certain that organised athletic contests were held in Greece some 3,500 years ago. There were at least four major Greek sporting festivals by the end of the 6th century BC, of which the Olympic Games, held in honour of Zeus, were the most famous. Held every four years between August 6 and September 19, they occupied such an important place in Greek life that time was measured by the interval between them – an Olympiad. Although the first Olympic champion listed in the records was one Coroebus of Elis, a cook, who won the sprint race in 776 BC, the Games were probably at least 500 years old at that time.

Like all Greek games, they were an intrinsic part of a religious festival. They were held at Olympia in the city-state of Elis, on a track about 27 metres wide and one stade, about 183 metres, long. Later, the word *stadion* sometimes described the *dromos* (a race one length of the track) and also the arena itself. The *dromos* was apparently the only event in 776 BC, but other events were added over the ensuing decades: longer races, wrestling, pentathlon, boxing, chariot racing, and events for boys. Further events were added from time to time, including contests for fully armed soldiers, heralds, and trumpeters. Women were not allowed as competitors or, except for the priestesses of Demeter, as spectators.

See OLYMPIC GAMES in volume 25 of the Macropaedia.

When was the first ombudsman appointed?

The post of ombudsman for civil affairs was created by the Swedish constitution of 1809. The holder of the office is appointed by Parliament, he enjoys complete independence and is responsible only to the law.

The Swedish ombudsman is entrusted with a general supervision over civil affairs, including the courts, the police, prisons, and the public administration, both central and local, but excluding ministers. He can act as a public prosecutor and as a receiver of complaints from aggrieved citizens. He can investigate jails, mental homes, homes for deliquent children, and retreats for alcoholics, to discover if they are administered in accordance with the law.

Apart from occasional prosecutions, the ombudsman has little positive power other than the right to inspect and demand the fullest information. But he is entitled to comment, to criticize, and to make recommendations as to the correct interpretation of the law. He can recommend the government to pay compensation to a claimant. He can expose maladministration. Only ministers and the king are immune from the scrutiny of the Swedish ombudsman.

See PUBLIC ADMINISTRATION in volume 26 of the Macropaedia.

Which paintings made Michelangelo superhuman?

Between the years 1508 and 1512, Michelangelo undertook the formidable task of decorating the ceiling of the Sistine Chapel for Pope Julius II. Under Julius' uncle Pope Sixtus IV, the chapel had been completed and the walls decorated with frescoes depicting scenes from the life of Moses and the life of Christ. Against his will Michelangelo was assigned to paint in fresco scenes from the creation, although he thought of himself as a sculptor.

He engaged a few of his former colleagues from the shop of Ghirlandajo and began with them to paint the "Drunkenness of Noah" above the entrance to the chapel. Michelangelo had little patience with his less gifted associates, dismissed them, and executed the entire ceiling alone. The scenes were painted in reverse chronological order, beginning with the "Drunkenness of Noah" over the door and ending with the act of creation over the altar.

The Sistine ceiling was recognised as a masterpiece in its own time. The artist was judged to be a superhuman being and earned the title "the divine Michelangelo".

See THE HISTORY OF WESTERN PAINTING in volume 25 of the Macropaedia.

What puzzles paleographers?

Paleography is the study of ancient and medieval handwriting. A paleographer must not only have a close acquaintance with the language of his texts. He must also be familiar with the writing materials of the day (papyrus or vellum for example) and with the various implements used for writing (rushes, reeds, metal pens, styluses, quills, and so on).

It is a European convention that writing starts on the left at the top and works line by line down the page. An eccentricity known as boustrophedon (from the Greek for "following the ox furrow"), whereby alternate lines are written backward in mirror writing, occurs chiefly in very ancient inscriptions.

Abbreviations are the principal problem confronting paleographers. Roman lawyers used them extensively to avoid repetition of technical terms. Abbreviations were also used in public inscriptions – e.g. IMP.(ERATOR), CAES.(AR). This use of abbreviation became even more common in medieval Latin. More than 13,000 abbreviation signs and devices are known.

In Greek and Roman times texts were written continuously, without space between the words. Copyists easily misread them. When Tacitus reported that some tribesmen went off to guard their own property: ADSVATVTANDA (*ad sua tutanda*), the copyist thought "Suatutanda" was a place and so this "ghost name" went into the geography books.

See HISTORY in volume 20 of the Macropaedia.

How long has man used paper?

Paper is the basic material for written communication and the dissemination of information. In addition paper and paperboard provide materials for hundreds of other uses, such as wrapping, packaging, towelling, insulating, and photography.

The word paper is derived from the reedy plant *papyrus*, which grows abundantly along the Nile River. Sheets made from layers of papyrus fibres dampened, pressed and so cemented together, were used as writing material in ancient times, and many papyrus records still survive.

Papermaking can be traced to about AD 105 in China. The art travelled slowly westward, reaching Samarkand in 751 and Baghdad in 793. By the 14th century a number of paper mills existed in Europe; the invention of printing in the 1450s bringing a vastly increased demand for paper. The work was done largely by hand, paper being made one sheet at a time until in 1798 Nicolas-Louis Robert built a moving screen belt that would deliver an unbroken sheet of paper. In the early 1800s Robert's ideas were developed in England, forming the basis for the modern mechanized papermaking industry.

See CHEMICAL PROCESS INDUSTRIES in volume 21 of the Macropaedia.

How are parachutes made?

The parachute was invented at virtually the same time as the balloon but independently from it. The principle had been recognized by several writers, including Leonardo da Vinci; it was first demonstrated in action in 1783. A jump from a balloon at about 2,400 metres was carried out in 1802.

Early parachutes were made of canvas; later, silk was employed. Modern man-carrying parachutes are made of nylon and assembled in a pack that contains the parachute canopy, a small pilot parachute that assists in opening the canopy, and suspension lines, attached to a harness worn by the user. The canopy is given extraordinary strength by fabrication from up to 28 separate panels, or gores, each made of smaller sections,

sewn together in such a way that a tear will usually be confined to the section in which it originates. The direction of the weave in each section adds further strength. The pack is fitted to the parachutist's back or front and opened by a ripcord that can be activated manually, by an automatic timing device, or by a line fastened to the aircraft. The harness is so constructed that deceleration, gravity, and wind forces are transmitted to the wearer's body with maximum safety and minimum discomfort.

See PARACHUTE in volume 9 of the Micropaedia.

Why do passerine birds follow ants?

The passerines, or perching birds, comprise the dominant and most highly evolved group of birds on Earth, with more than 5,000 species abundant on all continents except Antarctica and most oceanic islands. Passerines have evolved a great diversity of feeding adaptations. Of interest are the ways in which birds interact with ants. For example, in the New World, birds have become dependent on the huge troops of army ants which swarm over the forest floor, devouring all animal life in their path. The ant columns are accompanied by troops of birds that prey on the fleeing insects, spiders, lizards, and other creatures trying to escape the ants. Several antbirds are believed to be entirely dependent on army ants for finding food and some will follow large animals, including man, that stir up insects with their feet.

"Anting" is a peculiar ritual, still poorly understood, in which birds either pick up ants and wipe them on their feathers, or squat in a group of ants, allowing the ants to crawl into their feathers. This may be a form of feather-maintenance, since the ants exude or spray formic acid as a defensive fluid. This fluid is known to be insecticidal, and so dressing the feathers with ants tends to kill or deter parasites such as lice and mites.

See BIRDS in volume 15 of the Macropaedia.

How are cultured pearls produced?

Pearl farming is one of the most famous industries of Japan, dating to 1893, when a Japanese first succeeded in cultivating pearls. Under the skin of an oyster, the pearl farmer inserts a pearl nucleus (a small spherical shell fragment wrapped in a piece of living oyster tissue). The treated oyster is placed in a culture cage on a floating raft, and after a period of some months or years, the cultured oyster produces a pearl. Japan's pearl production centres, once scattered along the coast, are today concentrated in the Inland Sea.

See FISHING AND MARINE PRODUCTS in volume 19 of the Macropaedia.

Which birds provided the feathers for quill pens?

Quills were the principal writing instruments for more than 1,000 years. The best were obtained from living birds in the spring. Goose feathers were the principal source, quills from the scarcer, more expensive swan were preferred; but for fine lines, quills from crows were best.

See QUILL in volume 9 of the Micropaedia.

What makes Pepys' diary unique?

The diary by which Samuel Pepys (1633–1703) is chiefly known was kept between his 27th and 36th years. Written in Thomas Shelton's system of shorthand, with the names in longhand, it extends to 1,250,000 words, filling six quarto volumes.

It is far more than an ordinary record of its

writer's thoughts and actions; it is a supreme work of art, revealing on every page the capacity for selecting the small, as well as the large, essential that conveys the sense of life. One can open it on any page and lose oneself in the life of Charles II's London, and of this vigorous, curious, hardworking, pleasure-loving man. Pepys wanted to find out about everything because he found everything interesting. He never seemed to have a dull moment; he could not, indeed, understand dullness.

He described the Restoration and coronation; the horrors of the Plague; and the Fire of London, writing down his account – so strong was the artist in him – even as his home and its treasures were being threatened with destruction.

Pepys excluded nothing from his journal that seemed to him essential, however much it told against himself. He not only recorded his major infidelities and weaknesses; he put down all those little meannesses of thought and conduct of which all men are guilty but few admit, even to themselves. He possessed in a unique degree the quality of complete honesty.

See the biography of PEPYS in volume 9 of the Micropaedia.

Which English philosopher chose to be preserved in a glass case?

The philosopher and economist Jeremy Bentham (1748–1832) is known as the founder of the Utilitarian school. Bentham decided that mankind was governed by two sovereign motives, pain and pleasure. The object of all law-making must be "the greatest happiness of the greatest number." Bentham's views were respectfully received in France and America. Later he worked for prison reform and proposed a number of parliamentary reforms to bring about greater democracy. Bentham was less a philosopher than a critic of the law and of institutions – at this he was admirable, while his definitions of what he thought were the basic concepts of ethics are over-simple or ambiguous.

Bentham enjoyed a happy life, among congenial friends. After his death, in accordance with his instructions, his body was dissected in front of his friends. The skeleton was reconstructed, dressed in Bentham's clothes and (with a wax head) set in a glass-fronted case. It is still preserved in University College, London.

See the biography of BENTHAM in volume 2 of the Micropaedia

How do we choose our phobias?

Phobias are specific fears out of proportion to the apparent stimulus. Phobic reactions are given names that indicate the object or situation feared. Theoretically, the list of phobias could be endless; since some people fear specific numbers (*e.g.*, 3 or 7), the potential for specific number phobias (numerophobias) might be infinite. Some commonly encountered phobic reactions are

Acrophobia	heights
Agoraphobia	open spaces
Ailurophobia	cats
Anthophobia	flowers
Anthropophobia	people
Aquaphobia	water
Brontophobia	thunder
Claustrophobia	closed spaces
Cynophobia	dogs
Herpetophobia	lizards or reptiles
Mysophobia	dirt, germs, contamination

Numerophobia	a number or numbers
Nyctophobia	darkness or night
Ophidiophobia	snakes
Pyrophobia	fire

While phobic attacks are not uncommon in childhood, many of these tend to subside spontaneously. Phobias can develop at any age.

Psychoanalytic theorists consider the phobic object as an external representation of unconscious bases for fear and that one's "selection" of a phobic object is an unwitting process determined through symbolism or circumstantial influences. Thus, a child who has attacks of fear when he sees white horses may eventually learn through analysis that the horses symbolize his father, for whom he holds an unconscious (but unacceptable) fear.

See MENTAL DISORDERS in volume 23 of the Macropaedia.

Can a photograph be three-dimensional?

Holography is, in principle, a means of creating a unique photographic image without the use of a lens. The photographic recording of the image is called a hologram, which appears to be an unrecognizable pattern of stripes and whorls but which – when illuminated by coherent light, as by a laser beam – organizes the light into a three-dimensional representation of the original object.

An ordinary photographic image records the variations in intensity of light reflected from an object, producing dark areas where less light is reflected and light areas where more light is reflected. Holography, however, records not only the intensity of the light but also its phase, or the degree to which the wave fronts making up the reflected light are in step with each other, or coherent.

Dennis Gabor, Hungarian-born scientist, invented holography in 1948, and received the Nobel Prize for Physics for it in 1971.

See HOLOGRAPHY in volume 6 of the Micropaedia.

Of what use is a piezoelectric device?

Piezoelectricity is exploited in a variety of practical devices such as microphones, phonograph pick-ups, and wave filters in telephone-communications systems.

Pressure on certain electrically neutral crystals polarizes them by slightly separating the centre of positive charge from that of the negative charge; this separation may be described as a resultant electric field. Conversely, an electric field applied to a crystal will produce a mechanical deformation. A piezoelectric material, such as a thin slab of quartz, can convert a high frequency alternation signal to an ultrasonic wave of the same frequency. Or by the direct piezoelectric effect, such a crystal can convert a mechanical vibration, such as sound, into a corresponding electrical signal.

Piezoelectricity was discovered in 1880 by Pierre and Paul-Jacques Curie, but for several decades remained a laboratory curiosity. During World War I it was used in an early form of submarine-detecting sonar, and later found wide use in frequency control in radio communications. In World War II piezoelectric crystals were used in the detonators of air-dropped bombs; when the nose struck ground, the crystal sent a jolt of electricity to detonate the charge.

The piezoelectric effect has subsequently been used in much electronic equipment, in clocks and watches, cigarette lighters, and many other items.

See PIEZOELECTRICITY in volume 9 of the Micropaedia.

How many pipes does an organ have?

An organ is divided into three parts. At one end of the instrument are the keyboards, or manuals, and other controls that are collectively called the console. Between these two is the mechanism, or action, that accounts for a large part of the bulk and cost of any organ. The simplest type of organ has one keyboard and one pipe to each note, but since the tone of a pipe sounding on a constant pressure of wind is immutable, both as to quality and quantity, the uses of an organ with only one pipe to each note are limited. Even the smallest, therefore, have at least three pipes to each note, and organs of cathedral size commonly have as many as 100 to each note. These sets of pipes are arranged in parallel rows. The pallet controlled from each note admits wind to all the pipes belonging to that note; but in order that the organist may use at will all, none, or any of the sets of pipes, an intermediate mechanism is provided by which he may stop off any set or sets of pipes. The controls that operate this mechanism have come to be known as stops.

See MUSICAL INSTRUMENTS in volume 24 of the Macropaedia.

When might you meet a pixie?

A pixie, in the folklore of southwestern England, is a tiny elflike spirit or mischievous fairy who dances in the moonlight to the music of frogs and crickets; its favourite pastimes are leading travellers astray and frightening young maidens. Pixies also delight in rapping on walls, blowing out candles, and playing in water.

Their prank of leading people astray gave rise to the term pixie-led to describe a person who becomes lost on a familiar road. It was later extended to mean any state of bewilderment or confusion.

See PIXIE in volume 9 of the Micropaedia.

Which are the flattest plains on Earth?

Abyssal plains are exceedingly flat ocean-floor areas in depths of 3 to 6 kilometres, generally adjacent to continents. They vary in depth only 10 centimetres to one metre per kilometre of horizontal distance.

The plains are thought to be the upper surfaces of sediment that has come from the land. Seismic surveys have shown that the sediment averages one kilometre in thickness. It is made up of layers of coarse sediment that has flowed from the continental slopes, interbedded with fine-grained clay and the microscopic remains of organisms that inhabit the waters above. These fine-grained sediments are believed to fall through the water particle by particle, accumulating at rates of a millimetre to several centimetres per 1,000 years.

See ABYSSAL PLAINS in volume 1 of the Micropaedia.

Why do some plants explode?

Plants disperse their seeds in various ways – by wind, water, and animals, for example. Some are capable of self-dispersal. Best known in this category are the active ballists, which forcibly eject their seeds. In Scotch broom and gorse, drying of the already dead tissues in the two valves of the seed pod causes a tendency to warp. On summer days this culminates in an explosive and audible separation of these valves, with violent seed release. The plant champions in this form of seed dispersal include the sandbox tree, which can eject its seed to a distance of about 14 metres.

See REPRODUCTION AND REPRODUCTIVE SYSTEMS in volume 26 of the Macropaedia.

What changes have there been in the games children play?

Some children's games have been played for centuries. Swings existed on the island of Crete in 1600 BC, and jacks, or knucklebones, a game that involves tossing and then catching five or more jackstones, was played in ancient Greece. Both blindman's buff and a chase game date from 2,000 years ago. As social attitudes changed, some games became less popular, while others, especially those that involved violence towards animals, eventually disappeared. A few games became more structured and often lost their entertainment value.

Technological innovations have greatly influenced the history of children's games The discovery of rubber, for example, led to the creation of new types of balls, which in turn increased the number and frequency of ball games played. New cultural and trade ties introduced different toys such as the kite from China.

Manufactured games were originally used as a method of instruction beginning in the 17th century. The later development of geographical games, in which countries were cut out and children attempted to put them back correctly, led to the invention of the jigsaw puzzle. Many 19th-century games are still distributed, including snakes and ladders and ludo. Monopoly, developed in 1933, has become one of the most popular board games of all time.

See CHILDREN'S GAME in volume 3 of the Micropaedia.

Who dreamed of a play without words or actors?

Edward Gordon Craig (1872–1966) worked in three distinct yet overlapping areas of artistic endeavour: as actor, as director-designer, and, most important, as dramatic theorist.

His productions in the 1900s were marked by simplicity and unity of concept, with the emphasis being placed on the movement of actors and of light. Soon to come was the idea of moving scenery, which ultimately led to Craig's vision of a theatre without actors or words, in which the movement of scenery and of light would engender an emotional response in the audience.

He recorded his ideas through the medium of etching. His new theatrical concept was that the entire "scene" should be movable in all parts; both the floor and ceiling were to be composed of squares that, under the control of the artist, could be moved up and down independently or in groups within a constantly changing pattern of light. However, the financial support that would have permitted Craig to develop his ideas and to experiment was not forthcoming.

Many of Craig's "impractical" ideas have since become common practice; once a "rebel", he is now seen as a prophet. Even where modern technology has improved upon Craig's vision, the underlying aesthetic concept is still relevant.

See the article on CRAIG in volume 5 of the Macropaedia.

What writer's search for God led to his death by pneumonia?

Though happily married, famous as a novelist, and enjoying a large income, Tolstoy had become dissatisfied with himself by the time he finished *Anna Karenina.*

Ultimately he became convinced that the teachings of Christ contained the answer to his question about the meaning of life. His new convictions took a form of Christian anarchism that led him to reject the authority of the church, which in turn was to excommunicate him in

1901. He opposed organized government because it maintained itself through coercion, and he condemned private property because he believed that ownership was secured by force. He would have preferred to divest himself of his own property, but bowing to the wishes of his family, legally transferred his estate to them.

Tolstoy strove, by no means with complete success, to bring his daily life into conformity with his altered views. He abandoned smoking and drinking, became a vegetarian, and often dresssed in simple peasant clothes. The eloquence of his moral and religious writings, his fame, and his vital personality attracted many adherents, but his family had little sympathy for his new life. The worsening domestic situation finally caused him to leave home stealthily one night at the age of 82, with his doctor and his youngest daughter, in search of a refuge where he could live quietly and closer to God. A few days later at a remote railway junction he died of pneumonia.

See the biography of TOLSTOY in volume 28 of the Macropaedia.

Who was Pocahontas?

Pocahontas (*c.* 1595–1617) was a Powhatan Indian woman who helped maintain peace between

English colonists and native Americans by befriending the settlers at Jamestown, Virginia, and eventually marrying one of them.

Daughter of the powerful intertribal leader Powhatan, Pocahontas was a young girl when she first became acquainted with the colonists who settled in the Chesapeake Bay area in 1607. The following year she saved the life of Captain John Smith, founder and leader of the colony, after he had been captured by the tribe. Just as he laid his head on the sacrificial stone to await death, Pocahontas supposedly flung herself down and, embracing the captain's head, successfully implored her father to spare him.

Later, she was kidnapped by the colonists, who hoped to use her to negotiate permanent peace. She was ransomed by her father, but before she could return to her people she fell in love with John Rolfe, a distinguished settler, and they married. This union did indeed prove beneficial, and peace prevailed as long as Powhatan lived.

In 1616, Pocahontas and her husband went to England, where she was received at court and lionized by English society. About to embark for home, she contracted smallpox and died. Her only son, Thomas Rolfe, was educated in England and later migrated to Virginia, where he became a leading citizen.

See POCAHONTAS in volume 9 of the Micropaedia.

Who first published "pocket editions"?

Aldus Manutius, an Italian and the greatest printer-publisher of his time, began his printing business in 1490 with a series of Greek authors. He then hit on the idea of bringing out cheap "pocket editions" for the new readers produced by the Humanist movement. Beginning in 1501 and continuing with six titles a year for the next five years, he issued a series of Latin texts in octavo format that were models of scholarship and elegance. To keep down the cost, Aldus printed editions of 1,000, instead of the more usual 250; and to fill the page economically, he used an "italic" type designed for him by Francesco Griffo, another innovation of far-reaching effect.

The Aldine editions were widely copied, piratically and otherwise, and their dolphin and anchor was the first instance of a publisher's imprint that became a hallmark of excellence.

See PUBLISHING in volume 26 of the Macropaedia.

When was Paris ravaged by poisoners?

The "Affair of the Poisons" was one of the most sensational criminal cases of 17th-century France. In 1679 an inquiry revealed that nobles, prosperous bourgeois, and the common people alike had been resorting secretly to female fortune-tellers – at that time numerous in Paris – for drugs and poisons, for black masses, and for other criminal purposes.

A special tribunal for the trial of the accused was created in April 1679. It held 210 sessions, issued 319 writs of arrest, and sentenced 36 persons to death, including the poisoner La Voisin (Catherine Deshayes, Madame Monvoisin), who was burned on Feb. 22, 1680.

Among the many members of French society who were implicated was Madame de Montespan, the mistress of King Louis XIV. She was accused of being a customer of La Voisin from 1667; of resorting to magic and philtres to win the King's love; of participating in black masses; and also of attempting to poison her young rival, Mademoiselle de Fontanges, and the King himself.

See POISONS, AFFAIR OF THE in volume 9 of the Micropaedia.

How do poisons enable some plants and animals to survive?

The poisons produced by biological organisms are referred to as biotoxins, or biological poisons.

Poisonous plants and animals are found in greatest abundance and varieties in warm-temperate and tropical regions. Relatively few toxic organisms of any kind are found in polar latitudes.

Knowledge of the evolutionary significance and development of most biotoxins is largely speculative and poorly understood. In some instances they may have developed during the evolution of certain animal species as part of the food procurement mechanism. Biotoxins may also function as defensive mechanisms. The defense may be quite complex – as in the protection of territorial rights for reproductive purposes – and inhibitory or antibiotic substances may be produced that result in the exclusion of competitive animal or plant species. Certain marine organisms and terrestrial plants may release into the water, air, or soil inhibitory substances that discourage the growth of other organisms; examples include the production of antibiotic substances by micro-organisms.

Of increasing interest has been the discovery that certain substances which may be toxic to one group of organisms, may serve a vital function in the life processes of the source organism.

See POISONS AND POISONING in volume 25 of the Macropaedia.

How do porpoises play?

Play is common in toothed whales, such as dolphins and porpoises, but almost unknown in their cousins the baleen, or whalebone, whales. In porpoises, much play is sexual in nature, but they also balance sticks and other floating objects on their fins or flukes. Young whales will push small logs or planks. Fish may be thrown in the air or proferred to other fish lurking in crevices, apparently to lure them into the open. Porpoises swim and dive in groups, performing ballet-like movements, riding ocean swells or breaking surf in precise formation. Pilot whales have been seen resting head down, their tails in the air, or swimming on their backs.

Porpoises and dolphins live in tightly organized schools. Mother-young relationships persist for years, and school members will "stand by" a wounded animal or actually support a sick animal, sometimes one of a different species. Captive porpoises have mimicked human voice signals and other sounds. Their own acoustic behaviour includes echolocation, using low-pitched barks, whistles, screams, and moans, and high-pitched brief clicking noises. These sounds are used for social communication and for discrimination and navigation.

See MAMMALS in volume 23 of the Macropaedia.

What are "porridge pots"?

Although they are an aspect of volcanic activity, catastrophic eruptions represent only one part of the field and are generally of limited duration. A second and more common aspect of such activity consists of manifestations of more modest proportions, which are less spectacular but of great significance in the interpretation of volcanic eruptions.

Hot springs are common in all volcanic areas, even where the volcanoes are no longer active. They represent the last stage of heat loss by igneous (crystalline rock) masses beneath the Earth's surface, which continue to give off high temperature gases and vapours while cooling.

Geysers are spouting hot springs that throw forth intermittent jets of water and steam; fumaroles are steam vents named from the Latin word *fumus*, "smoke": the smoke is water vapour. Within this group are included the paint pots, porridge pots, and mud volcanoes, all of which are hot springs of limited water supply and acid reaction. Their immediately adjacent surface rocks are undergoing active chemical attack from magmatic steam and acid gases to provide the porridge, whereas the iron content of the rocks provides the paint. Another related form, the Mofettes (German *Muff*, "musty smell"), mark the very last stage of volcanic activity.

See VOLCANISM in volume 29 of the Macropaedia.

Could you post a letter in 2000 BC?

Since good communications were clearly essential for governing the extensive empires of the ancient world, it is not surprising that the earliest historical references to postal systems should concern Egypt about 2000 BC and China under the Chou dynasty 1,000 years later. It was probably in China that a posthouse relay system was first developed and was brought to a high state of development under the Mongol emperors. The great Persian Empire of Cyrus in the 6th century BC also employed relays of mounted messengers, served by posthouses.

The development of Rome from a small city-state into a vast empire embracing most of the known world brought with it the necessity for reliable and speedy communication with the governors of distant provinces. This need was met by the *cursus publicus*, the most highly developed postal system of the ancient world.

The political fragmentation of Europe caused all traces of the Roman postal system to disappear. The *cursus publicus* fared better in the Eastern Empire because its provinces were eventually absorbed into the Islamic Empire. The substitution of one imperial regime for another meant that the *cursus publicus* could be incorporated into a postal system based in Baghdad.

See POSTAL SYSTEMS in volume 25 of the Macropaedia.

How did the Chinese decorate their pottery?

Nowhere in the world has pottery assumed such importance as in China, and the influence of

Chinese porcelain on later European pottery has been profound.

Chinese decoration is usually symbolic and often exploits the double meaning of certain words; for instance, the Chinese word for bat, *fu*, also means "happiness". Five bats represent the Five Blessings – longevity, wealth, serenity, virtue, and an easy death. The "Buddha's hand" citron, a fruit with finger-like appendages, is a symbol of wealth, and each month and season is represented by a flower or plant. The *pa kua*, consisting of eight sets of three lines, broken and unbroken in different combinations, represent natural forces, and are often seen in conjunction with the Yin-Yang symbol, which represents the male-female principle. The dragon is generally a mild and beneficent creature. It is a symbol of the emperor, just as a phoenix-like creature symbolizes the empress.

Of the three principal religious systems in China, Confucianism, Taoism, and Buddhism, Taoist figures, in particular, appear frequently on porcelain as decoration.

See Decorative Arts and Furnishings in volume 17 of the Macropaedia.

What industry did public criers start?

The first advertising was by public criers in ancient times who walked through the streets calling attention to the sale of such items as slaves, cattle, and imported goods. An ancient written advertisement, perhaps 3,000 years old, was discovered by an archaeologist delving in the ruins of Thebes. It offered "a whole gold coin" as reward for the return of a runaway slave named Shem.

Printing made possible the transition from simple announcement to the system of argument and suggestion that constitutes modern advertising. The medium of this development was the newspaper. The weekly newspapers carried a few advertisements including the first offers of coffee (1652), chocolate (1657), and tea (1658) in England. In 1666 the *London Gazette* announced the first advertisement supplement: "An Advertisement – Being daily prest to the publication of Books, Medicines and other things not properly the business of a Paper of Intelligence. This is to notifie once for all, that we will not charge the *Gazette* with Advertisements, unless they be matters of state: but that a Paper of Advertisements will be forthwith printed apart . . ."

Advertising was prospering in the following century, and in 1758 Samuel Johnson could write in *The Idler*: "Advertisements are now so numerous that they are very negligently perused, and it is therefore become necessary to gain attention by magnificence of promise and by eloquence sometimes sublime and sometimes pathetick."

See Marketing and Merchandising in volume 23 of the Macropaedia.

Who built the Pyramids of Egypt?

The Pyramids of Giza stand on a plateau on the west bank of the Nile near al-Jīzah. The northernmost and oldest of the group was built by Khufu (Cheops in Greek), the second king of the 4th dynasty. Called the Great Pyramid, it is the largest of the three, the length of each side at the base averaging 270 metres. The middle pyramid was built by Khafre (Greek Chephren), the fourth of the eight kings of the 4th dynasty. The southernmost and last pyramid to be built was that of Menkaure (Greek Mycerinus), the sixth king of the 4th dynasty.

All three pyramids were plundered both internally and externally; and thus, most of the grave goods are missing, and the pyramids no longer reach their original height.

Each monument originally consisted of not

only the pyramid itself, which housed the body of the deceased king, but also an adjoining mortuary temple and a sloping causeway leading from this temple to a valley temple near the Nile.

See GIZA, PYRAMIDS OF in volume 5 of the Micropaedia.

Who broadcast a radio program in 1906?

On Christms Eve, 1906, a radio program made up of two musical selections, the reading of a poem and a short talk was broadcast by Reginald Aubrey Fessenden from his experimental station at Brant Rock, Massachusetts. It was heard by ship wireless operators within a radius of several hundred kilometres. The first commercial radio station in the United States went on the air in Pittsburgh on November 2, 1920 with the returns of the presidential election.

The first successful broadcasting of the human voice across the Atlantic, from a transmitter in Ireland, led to the erection of a transmitter at Chelmsford in England. Two daily half-hour programs of speech and music, including a broadcast by the opera singer Dame Nellie Melba, were broadcast for about a year between 1919 and 1920.

After the Chelmsford broadcasts were banned by the Post Office, thousands of radio amateurs petitioned for regular broadcasts, and the Marconi Company was allowed to broadcast about 15 minutes weekly. The first of these authorized broadcasts, from a hut at Writtle close to Chelmsford, took place on February 14, 1922. Later that year the British Broadcasting Company was formed.

See BROADCASTING in volume 15 of the Macropaedia.

What musical styles influenced ragtime?

Ragtime evolved in the playing of honky-tonk pianists along the Mississippi and Missouri rivers in the last decades of the 19th century; it was influenced by minstrel-show songs, blacks' banjo styles, and syncopated (off-beat) dance rhythms of the cakewalk, and also by elements of European music. Ragtime found its characteristic expression in formally structured piano compositions. The regularly accented left-hand beat, in $^4{}_4$ or $^2{}_4$ time, was opposed in the right hand by a fast, bouncingly syncopated melody that gave the music its powerful forward impetus.

Ragtime was one forerunner of jazz and the predominant style of U.S. popular music from about 1899 to 1917.

See RAGTIME in volume 9 of the Micropaedia.

How was Ramses II saved from the waters of the Nile?

Four colossal statues of the Egyptian king Ramses II at Abu Simbel are one of the most spectacular examples of ancient Egyptian art, unknown to the outside world until their rediscovery in 1813.

The 20-metre seated figures were carved out of a sandstone cliff on the west bank of the Nile, two on either side of the entrance to a main temple extending 56 metres into the cliff. It was built so that on certain days of the year the first rays of the morning sun would penetrate its whole length and even illuminate the shrine in its innermost sanctuary. Just to the north of the main temple was a smaller one, adorned with smaller statues.

When the reservoir created by the Aswan High Dam threatened to submerge Abu Simbel in the early 1960s, UNESCO and the Egyptian government sponsored a project to save the site. A work force and an international team of engineers and scientists, supported by funds from more than 50 countries, dug away the top of the cliff and completely disassembled both temples. They were reconstructed on high ground 60 metres above the river bed.

See ABU SIMBEL in volume 1 of the Micropaedia.

What did prehistoric man use as a razor?

Prehistoric cave drawings show that clam shells, shark's teeth, and sharpened flints were used as shaving implements, and flints are still in use by certain primitive tribes. Solid gold and copper razors have been found in Egyptian tombs of the 4th millennium BC. According to the Roman historian Livy, the razor was introduced in Rome in the 6th century BC by Lucius Tarquinius Priscus, legendary king of Rome; but shaving did not become customary until the 5th century BC.

See RAZOR in volume 9 of the Micropaedia.

Reynard the Fox: hero or villain?

The fox appears as the hero of several medieval cycles of tales in verse that satirize contemporary human society. Reynard the fox, sly and cowardly

though he be, is still a sympathetic figure. He symbolizes the triumph of craft over brute strength (as personified by the dull-witted wolf in the stories).

Many of the tales are French, though the stories are found all over the world. They were so popular that in France the nickname *renard* replaced the old word for fox, *goupil*.

See REYNARD THE FOX in volume 10 of the Micropaedia.

Was there a real Robin Hood?

Robin Hood was the hero of a series of English ballads, some of which date from at least the 14th century. He was a rebel, and many of the most striking episodes in the tales about him show him and his companions robbing and killing representatives of authority. Their most frequent enemy is the sheriff of Nottingham, a local agent of central government.

Numerous attempts have been made to prove that there was a historical Robin Hood, though references to the legend by medieval writers make it clear that the ballads themselves were the only evidence for his existence available to them. A popular modern belief that he was of the time of Richard I probably stems from a "pedigree" fabricated by an 18th-century antiquary, Richard Stukely.

A more serious view has been advanced that he was one of the disinherited followers of Simon de Montfort, after the latter's defeat in 1265.

See ROBIN HOOD in volume 10 of the Micropaedia.

What did the Romans think of dancing?

Roman antagonism to dance seems to reflect a sober rationalism and realism. Nonetheless, Rome did not entirely evade its temptations. Before about 200 BC, dances were evidently in the form of choral processions only. There were agricultural processions led by priests, and weapon dances of the Salii, a congregation of the priests of Mars who walked around in a circle rhythmically beating their shields.

Later, Greek and Etruscan influences began to spread, though people who danced were considered suspicious, effeminate, and even dangerous by the Roman nobility. One public official did not believe his eyes when he watched dozens of the daughters and sons of well-respected Roman patricians and citizens enjoying themselves in a dancing school. About 150 BC all dancing schools were ordered closed, but the trend could not be stopped. And though the dance may have been alien to the Romans' inner nature, dancers and dancing teachers were increasingly brought from abroad in the following years. The statesman and scholar Cicero summed up the general opinion of the Romans when he stated that no man danced unless he was insane.

See THE HISTORY OF WESTERN DANCE in volume 16 of the Macropaedia.

How did the "ropers" catch their "mark"?

By the early 1900s, huge payoffs in confidence games attracted the interest of racketeers, particularly in the United States. Elaborate schemes were devised in order to exploit sophisticated and wealthy victims.

"Ropers", posing as rich financiers, industrialists, and millionaire sportsmen, began travelling the world in search of "marks", or victims. A popular swindle, known as past posting, required a dummy telegraph office, used to persuade the mark that horse-race results could be delayed long enough for him to bet on the winner after the race was won. As soon as the mark committed a large amount of money, sometimes as much as $250,000, the operators disappeared.

Confidence games continue to flourish, primarily because prominent victims rarely report them, for fear of being prosecuted for their own complicity in a criminal activity.

See CONFIDENCE GAME in volume 3 of the Micropaedia.

Why do roadrunners jaywalk?

The road runner is a ground-dwelling relative of the cuckoo that lives in the deserts of Mexico and the southwestern U.S. It is about 55 centimetres long, with streaked brown and white plumage, bare blue and red skin behind the eyes, stout bluish legs, and long, graduated tail carried at an upward angle. Clumsy in flight and quickly tiring, the bird usually prefers to run along roads or across sagebrush, chaparral, or mesquite flats. It feeds on insects, lizards, and snakes.

See ROADRUNNER in volume 10 of the Micropaedia.

Why do we eat salt?

Salt, sodium chloride, is essential to the health of men and animals. Nomads, who live mainly on milk and raw or roasted meat (in which natural salts are not lost) never eat additional salt with their food. On the other hand, peoples with largely cereal, vegetable, or boiled meat diets, require extra salt. In parts of central Africa, salt is still a luxury available only to the rich. The use of salt is intimately connected with the advance from nomadic to agricultural life. The gods were worshipped as the givers of the kindly fruits of the earth, and salt was usually included in offerings. Salt was a necessary element in sacrificial meals, and its preservative qualities made it a fitting symbol of an enduring compact.

The word salt thus acquired connotations of high esteem and honour in many languages, ancient and modern. Examples are the Arab "There is salt between us" and in English, the phrase "salt of the earth" describing a person held in high esteem. One of the oldest roads in Italy is the Via Salaria or "Salt Route" over which Roman salt was carried into other parts of Italy.

Cakes of salt have been used as money in Ethiopia and elsewhere in Africa and in Tibet. In the Roman army an allowance of salt was made to officers and men; in imperial times, this *salarium* was converted into an allowance of money – hence the English word "salary".

See FOOD PROCESSING in volume 19 of the Macropaedia.

Why is the saxophone so called?

The saxophone, a single-reed instrument made of metal, was invented by Antoine-Joseph Sax (1814–1894), a Belgian working in Paris. The new instrument resulted from Sax's efforts to improve the tone of the bass clarinet and was patented in 1846. Other instruments invented by Sax and his father Charles Joseph (who worked with him) were the saxhorn, the saxotromba and the saxtuba. Later Sax taught saxophone at the Paris Conservatoire, but, like so many inventors, he failed to profit from the commercial exploitation of his work and ended his life in poverty.

See SAX, ANTOINE-JOSEPH in volume 10 of the Micropaedia.

What was the "Scopes Trial"?

In 1925 in Dayton, Tennessee, a high school teacher named John T. Scopes was charged with violating state law. His offence, which he admitted, was to teach the theory of evolution – banned

by Tennessee's legislature that same year. Scopes was defended (unsuccessfully) by the lawyer Clarence Darrow, convicted and fined $100. He was subsequently acquitted on a technicality. The law was repealed, though not until 1967.

See Scopes Trial in volume 10 of the Micropaedia.

How long have we known what's at the bottom of the sea?

Until recently, only very crude data about the depths of seawater and the character of the sea bottom were available. Observations of the British "Challenger" expedition from 1872 to 1876 provided the first soundings and samples from the ocean bottom, but these were too infrequent to provide a serious picture. The development of echo-sounding devices in the early 1920s showed, for the first time, the actual irregularities of the seabed, and only since World War II has enough information been gathered to provide reliable ocean-floor maps.

Among the important practical benefits that promise to accumulate from undersea exploration are more efficient use of the potential food supply, new sources of pharmacological materials, and mineral resources, including not only oil and gas but hard minerals. Salt, bromine, and magnesium are already being economically extracted. The seabed may also yield coal, potash, phosphatic rock, iron ore, bauxite, and possibly metallic vein deposits. Coal has already been mined from onshore shafts or artificial islands off the coasts of Canada, the United Kingdom, Japan, and Taiwan. The nodules and crusts that rise in certain places in the deep ocean contain manganese, copper, cobalt, and nickel.

See Exploration in volume 19 of the Macropaedia.

How do sharks find their prey?

Sharks, though often said to have a low order of intelligence, have survived successfully over a long period of geologic time. They rely principally on their highly developed sense of smell to locate food. Given a favourable direction of current, sharks can detect incredibly minute concentrations of certain substances in the water, such as blood. Their hearing too is sensitive, particularly to sounds of low frequency but their eyesight is more limited. Taste buds in the shark's mouth enable it to distinguish and discriminate in its choice of food. Several species tested preferred tuna, for example, to other fish species. However, at times sharks become less fastidious and in a feeding frenzy will attack anything, including others of their own kind.

Sharks and their close relations, the rays, figure prominently in marine folklore and art. Among the known shark species, 27 have been authoritatively implicated in attacks on persons or boats. The great majority of such attacks occur in warm water, but unfortunately this rule does not apply to the great white shark or man-eater (*Carcharodon carcharias*) which ranges into cooler waters. Size is no criterion, for man-eaters become dangerous when only about a metre long and the largest ones, the basking shark and whale shark, which grow to 12 and 18 metres respectively, are harmless plankton-eaters.

See Fishes in volume 19 of the Macropaedia.

How did sailing ships survive the age of steam?

In 1775 the first successful trial of a boat driven by steam, on the Seine by Jacques Périer, foreshadowed the end of the age of sail. The sailing vessel fought long and hard, not admitting defeat for 100 years or more. One diehard Finnish skipper, Capt. Gustaf Ericson, who sailed in the 1920s and 1930s, built up a fleet of 16 sailing ships, ran them uninsured, except for their cargoes, and manned them with boys in training.

There are still more than 80 big square-riggers sailing the seas today. One or two serve as yachts or commercial pleasure ships, but nearly all the others are used to train youngsters for the navy or the mercantile marine of 18 different nations. Several have been built and launched since World War II.

See TRANSPORTATION in volume 28 of the Macropaedia.

When was shorthand first used?

Shorthand is a method of writing rapidly by substituting characters, abbreviations, or symbols for letters, words, or phrases. The Greek historian Xenophon used an ancient Greek system of shorthand to write the memoirs of Socrates. It was in the Roman Empire, however, that shorthand first became generally used. Marcus Tullius Tiro, a learned freedman in Cicero's household, invented the first Latin shorthand system in 63 BC. It lasted over a thousand years.

In the middle ages in Europe shorthand became associated with witchcraft and magic, and disappeared, although Thomas Becket was interested in Tiro's system and in the 15th century interest in shorthand revived. Timothy Bright invented an English system in 1588. Modern systems date from the 19th century. Pitman shorthand, for example, was published in 1837; Gregg shorthand in 1888.

While of obvious use in recording the proceedings of legislative bodies, court testimony, or dictation in business correspondence, shorthand has been used through the centuries as a cultural tool. Samuel Pepys recorded his diary in shorthand, and George Bernard Shaw wrote his plays in shorthand.

See WRITING in volume 29 of the Macropaedia.

Should we have sympathy for snakes?

Snakes are a widely known and much misunderstood group of animals. Arms and legs gone, no ears, only one working lung, voiceless, eyelids missing – a human being in such a condition would be under constant care. Snakes have not only survived but also become highly successful predators – fearless, independent, and usually solitary. Apart from hunting, most of a snake's time is dedicated to continued survival in an antagonistic world that is usually either too hot or too cold and is full of other organisms challenging the snake's right to live.

After the unfortunate episode of the Garden of Eden, perhaps the first relationship between man and snakes that one thinks of is snakebite. However of 1,000 bites in the United States each year, only approximately 15 result in death. Records of bites by the viper in England indicate that only seven deaths occurred between 1899 and 1945.

No snake has ever regularly hunted man, but man continues to engage in seeking out snakes. When man moves in, practically all reptiles share the fate of large animals and predatory birds – they must move out or die. Of the reptiles, the snake is the most distasteful to man, and snakes are quickly wiped out. The penalty for this eradication is an increase in the natural prey of snakes, including rats, mice, and other rodents.

Snakes cannot feed in cold weather. They must seek out a safe place where they can be completely inactive. Good dens for hibernation are few and far between and so attract many snakes, often of different species. At the end of the cold season, the snake cannot rouse itself. It is totally dependent upon the changes in its surroundings to bring it back to activity. It cannot mate until the sun's rays have warmed it, allowing it to take a renewed interest in life.

See REPTILES in volume 26 of the Macropaedia.

How does soap clean?

The seemingly simple process of cleaning a soiled surface is, in fact, a complex one, and consists of the following steps:

1. Wetting of the surface and, in the case of textiles, penetration of the fabric by the solution containing the detergent. Detergents increase the spreading and wetting ability of the water by reducing its surface tension, that is, the affinity its molecules have for each other in preference to the molecules of the material to be washed.

2. Absorption of a layer of soap or detergent between the water and the surface to be washed and between the water and the soil.

3. Dispersion of the soil into the wash water; this is facilitated by mechanical agitation and high temperature.

4. Preventing the soil from being deposited

again on to the surface cleaned. This is accomplished by suspending the dirt in a protective colloid, sometimes with the aid of special additives; for proteinic stains such as egg, milk, and blood, enzymes that break down protein must be used.

See CHEMICAL PROCESS INDUSTRIES in volume 21 of the Macropaedia.

Are the Spanish Steps really French?

One of the most striking architectural elements in all Rome is the renowned Scala di Spagna (Spanish Steps, or Stairs) in the Piazza di Spagna.

The staircase is a rare case of the failure of French cultural propaganda, for while they are called the Spanish Steps – the Spanish Embassy moved onto the square in the 17th century – they are unequivocally French. First suggested by the French about the time the Spanish Embassy was being installed, the idea was approved by papal authorities 100 years later and paid for with a legacy from a French diplomat. The stairs ascend to the French-built church and convent of Trinità dei Monti.

Charles Dickens described the steps as thronged with unengaged "artist's models" in regional costume. They are still crowded with loiterers in distinctive dress, students from all over the world. Since the end of the 16th century, the Piazza di Spagna has been a stopping place for tourists. Young lords on the Grand Tour of Europe left their heavy touring coaches for refitting in a side street still called Via delle Carozze (Carriage Street). The room on the piazza in which John Keats died in 1821 has been made into a museum.

See ROME in volume 26 of the Macropaedia.

What were spices first used for?

The most notable uses of spices and herbs in very early times were in medicine, in the making of holy oils and unguents, and as aphrodisiacs. Priests employed them in worship, incantations, magical rites, and rituals.

Ancient herbals, including those of Cathay, Sumer, Assyria, Egypt, Greece, and Rome, testify to the use of spices and herbs in the treatment of disease. Hippocrates, Galen, and Pedanius Dioscorides, among others, employed them. In the first century of the Christian Era, Pliny the Elder, in his *Natural History*, extols at length the efficacy and healing powers of spices and herbs in the treatment of just about every ailment known in his day.

It is not known when man first used spices and herbs in food. Sesame seems to have been known and employed as food, for making wine, and for its oil from time immemorial. Certainly by the time of the ancient Greeks and Romans many spices and herbs had come into use to flavour food and beverages.

In Europe, knowledge slowly spread of the use of spices and herbs to aid in the preservation of food by slowing or preventing rancidity and to flavour dishes. By medieval times large quantities of culinary herbs were in use. Eastern spices were beyond the purse of the greater number of people, but with the ascendancy of the western European nations in the Oriental spice trade the aromatic and pungent spices finally came into general use by rich and poor alike.

See SPICE AND HERB in volume 11 of the Micropaedia.

Where does the spider emulate the hare?

The best known type of African folk tale is the animal-trickster story. In East, Central, and South Africa, the trickster is the hare; in West Africa the spider or the tortoise. The trickster often uses his ingenuity to gratify his greed and satisfy his ill will. But he enjoys the audience's sympathy because by his trickery he usually defeats bigger and stronger animals.

The Yoruba of Nigeria poke fun at their own faults when they tell stories of the tortoise-trickster. Sometimes his cunning defeats itself, as when the tortoise steals from the gods a calabash that contains all the wisdom in the world. He hangs it round his neck but when he comes to a tree trunk lying across the road, he is unable to get over it because the calabash gets in his way. In his anxiety he fails to think of putting it on his back. Frustrated, the tortoise smashes the calabash, and so, ever since that day, wisdom has been scattered over all the world in tiny pieces.

A variant of the trickster story is the escape story, in which the hero extricates himself from an impossible task by imposing an impossible condition. One such story tells how a cruel king of Benin ordered his subjects on pain of death to build a new palace, but to start at the top and build downward. All were in despair until one wise old man went to the King and said that they were now ready to begin and would he, according to tradition, come and lay the foundation stone?

See AFRICAN ARTS in volume 13 of the Macropaedia.

What was "spontaneous generation"?

Among the many ideas advanced to answer the question "How did life originate?" was the Greek belief in spontaneous generation. According to this theory, living things could originate from non-living matter. The Greeks thought that flies and other small animals arose from the mud at the bottom of streams and ponds. The invention of the microscope, however, revealed the existence of a densely populated but previously invisible world of organisms still to be explained.

A 17th-century Italian, Francesco Redi, observed the development of maggots and flies on decaying meat. He demonstrated that if flies were excluded from the meat, maggots did not develop. On meat exposed to air, however, eggs laid by flies developed into maggots. The notion of spontaneous generation was not finally dismissed however until the 1860s, when Louis Pasteur showed by experiment that micro-organisms develop in suitable media from micro-organisms in the air and not from the air itself.

See BIOLOGICAL SCIENCES in volume 14 of the Macropaedia.

How are stadiums the forerunners of the cities of the future?

The stadium is a unique form of structure with an exceptionally significant role in 20th-century construction technology.

A basic difficulty of the roofed stadium was the interference with visibility by the columns supporting the roof. An important new development was the application of flexible steel cables to span large roof dimensions. In 1956 Lev Zetlin, a U.S. engineer, developed a rigid cable system since used on many arenas.

The concept of an enclosed stadium and the desire for greater capacities have led toward the search for improved materials and construction techniques. Modern technology, including that developed in the aerospace industry, already possesses techniques for covering very large spans. Such is the potential of the modern stadium design concept that architects and engineers view the roofed stadiums of the 20th century as the forerunners of completely roofed, weather-controlled cities.

See STADIUM in volume 11 of the Micropaedia.

What was lost when stained glass became more perfect?

Rarely equalled and never surpassed, the great stained-glass windows of the 12th and early 13th centuries actually predate significant technical advances in the glassmaker's craft by more than half a century. Whether by accident or by deliberate intent, the glass made in the 12th and 13th centuries had almost the ideal combination of crudity and refinement for stained glass. The sheets, 25 by 30 centimetres in size, were both flat enough and thin enough to be cut very accurately into the necessary shapes, yet still variable enough in thickness to have rich transitions in the depth of their colours.

With the progress of glass technology in the Middle Ages and Renaissance came the ability to produce larger, thinner, and flatter sheets of glass in a considerably larger range of colours than had been possible in the 13th century. At each distinguishable stage in this development, however, the glass became less visually interesting as an aesthetic element in its own right. The Gothic Revivalists later realized this, and in the mid-19th century they initiated a return to the earlier methods of producing glass. They developed the so-called "antique" glass, which is remarkably similar in colour, texture, and shading to that used in the 12th and 13th century.

See DECORATIVE ARTS AND FURNISHINGS in volume 17 of the Macropaedia.

How do starfish use their arms?

Starfish are echinoderms, and many are active predators on shellfishes and even on others of their own kind. They use their tube feet to pull apart the shells of their prey, Like other echinoderms, starfish can regenerate new arms if existing ones are broken off. This ability frustrated early attempts to keep starfishes from destroying commercial oyster beds; when captured starfishes were chopped into pieces and thrown back into the sea, they actually increased in numbers.

Starfish have an unusual method of feeding. They extrude their stomach through the mouth onto the prey, which is then partially digested externally, after which the stomach is eventually retracted and digestion is completed inside the body. When turned upside down, a starfish uses its feet and arms to perform a slow graceful somersault to restore itself to a normal position.

See ECHINODERMS in volume 17 of the Macropaedia.

How empty is space?

The atmosphere of the Earth may be considered to extend to an altitude of 160 kilometres above the Earth's surface. Such a distance is infinitesimal in comparison with the immensity of the universe. Even within the solar system, distances between planets are measured in tens of millions of kilometres. The distance to Pluto, the Sun's outermost planet, is more than 4,800,000,000 kilometres. The Earth's nearest neighbouring stars lie more than four light-years (about 40,000,000,000,000 kilometres) away.

This apparent unimaginable void of space, however, is not empty. Throughout these vast reaches, matter (largely hydrogen) is scattered at the extremely low density of perhaps ten particles per cubic centimetre in interplanetary space and one particle per cubic centimetre in interstellar space. Additionally, space is permeated by gravitational fields and a wide spectrum of electromagnetic radiation, by cosmic rays and magnetic fields of unknown intensities and distributions.

See EXPLORATION in volume 19 of the Macropaedia.

Which composer is said to have committed suicide by cholera?

Peter Ilich Tchaikovsky completed his *Symphony No. 6 in B Minor*, Opus 74, which was his last and which he rightly regarded as a masterpiece, in August 1893. In October he conducted its first performance in St. Petersburg but was disappointed with its reception. Its novel slow finale could hardly have been expected to induce such applause as had greeted, only 1½ years before, the première of the lighter *Nutcracker* suite. Yet perversely, Tchaikovsky did expect it and was determined to make an issue of it with himself. Into this work, with its "secret" program, he had put his whole soul, and the public did not appreciate it.

A aura of mystery surrounded Tchaichovsky's death. The story circulated at the time of his death was that he drank a glass of unboiled water during the cholera epidemic that was sweeping St. Petersburg and died of the disease. Whether or not this was the case, the rumour was soon rife that he had committed suicide as a result of the failure of his last symphony, whose very title, *Pathétique*, if nothing else, was enough to ensure it instant notoriety.

See the article on TCHAIKOVSKY in volume 11 of the Micropaedia.

When was sugar listed with precious stones?

Sugar making was known in India as early as 3000 BC. The methods of growing cane and making sugar were propagated from India east to Indochina and west to the Arabian countries and Europe. By the 8th century, sugarcane was grown and sugar made in Arabic Spain and southern France.

In 1493, on his second voyage, Christopher Columbus took sugarcane to the New World. The success of sugar plantations in Santo Domingo led to its cultivation in other islands of the West Indies.

Venice was long the chief centre of sugar refining in Europe, supplanted in the 16th century by Antwerp. In 1544 two refineries were established in London and in 1698 one in New York.

Sugar was initially dispensed medicinally as a sedative. As a food or food sweetener it was a scarce luxury until the 17th century. It remained expensive as late as 1736, when it was listed with precious stones among the wedding gifts of Maria Theresa, future queen of Hungary.

The sugar beet grew wild in parts of Asia and was cultivated at an early time in southern Europe as well as in Egypt. It was long used as a garden vegetable and cattle fodder. The world's first beet-sugar factory began operations in 1802 at Cunern, Silesia. By 1810 it was evident that beet sugar could be the basis for a successful industry.

See FOOD PROCESSING in volume 19 of the Macropaedia.

How does suggestion help advertisers?

In psychology, suggestion is the name given to the process of leading a person to respond uncritically, as in belief or action. The mode of suggestion, though usually verbal, may be visual or may involve any other sense.

Most advertisements involve direct suggestion

– asking or telling people to buy a product, often because a famous person uses or recommends it (prestige suggestion) or because most people buy it (social suggestion). Subliminal stimulation, the presentation of stimuli too faint or too brief to be consciously perceived, has been offered as an example of indirect suggestion; for example, although the claim has been disputed, popcorn sales were reported to increase by subliminal suggestion via the cinema screen.

Physiological factors such as disease, malnutrition and drugs may increase suggestibility but are of relative unimportance in daily life. Brainwashing techniques demonstrate the part such conditions may play in suggestibility. Hypnosis also increases suggestibility, although not as much as might be supposed – the subject will not perform acts contrary to his normal moral code.

See SUGGESTION in volume 11 of the Micropaedia.

What was the Aztec myth of the "Suns"?

The Aztecs believed, as did other Middle American Indians, that four worlds had existed before the present universe. These worlds or "Suns" had been destroyed by catastrophes. Mankind had been entirely wiped out at the end of each Sun. The present world was the fifth Sun.

Present mankind was created by Quetzalcóatl (the god in the shape of the "feathered snake"), who succeeded in reviving the dried bones of the old dead by sprinkling them with his own blood. The present Sun is doomed to disappear in a tremendous Earthquake, after which skeleton-like monsters of the west will appear and kill all mankind.

Two deeply rooted concepts are revealed by these myths. One is the belief that the universe is unstable, that death and destruction continually threaten it. The other emphasizes the necessity of the sacrifice of the gods. Thanks to Quetzalcóatl's self-sacrifice, the ancient bones of Mictlan, "the Place of Death", have given birth to men.

See PRE-COLUMBIAN CIVILIZATIONS in volume 26 of the Macropaedia.

How heavy is a supernova?

A supernova is a violently exploding star whose luminosity suddenly increases from hundreds of thousands to hundreds of millions of times its normal level after eruption. A supernova explosion is a cataclysmic event for a star, one that essentially ends its active (*i.e.* energy-generating) lifetime. When a star "goes supernova", considerable amounts of its matter, equalling the material of several Suns, may be blasted into space with such a burst of energy as to enable the exploding star to outshine its entire home galaxy consisting of hundreds of billions of stars.

One of the two types of supernovae has as progenitor a heavyweight star of at least eight solar masses that is at the end of its active lifetime. An iron core has built up at the very centre of the aging star. When this becomes too massive, it can no longer resist the tremendous pull of gravity and it collapses into a hard, rapidly spinning core. The core is composed almost entirely of neutrons, which are compressed in a volume only 10 kilometres across but whose combined weight equals that of several Suns. A teaspoonful of this extraordinarily dense material would weigh 50,000,000,000 tons on Earth. Detonation occurs when material falls in from the outer layers and rebounds off the core.

See SUPERNOVA in volume 11 of the Micropaedia.

What is the difference between plane and geodetic surveying?

The objective of all surveying – whether plane or geodetic – is to determine accurately land or water areas and their boundaries. Related data sought, also determined through surveys, include depths, altitudes, rate of slope (especially useful in mines and tunnel work), and earth volumes such as required for construction. Thus the surveyor specializes in the measurement of distances and directions, both horizontal and vertical.

In contrast to other types of measurement, nearly all those in surveying are made either perpendicular to the direction of gravity (designated as horizontal) or in the direction of gravity (designated as vertical). Horizontal lengths, with few exceptions, are measured in short, straight sections that are together very nearly arcs along the Earth's curved surface.

Within any area of the Earth's suface about 20 kilometres square and free of large variations in altitude, the differences between measurements made in relation to gravity and the same measurements that might be reproduced on, or from, a truly plane surface would be negligible because the differences caused by the Earth's curvature in a small area are minimal. The results of such surveys can be computed by plane trigonometry; the whole process is called plane surveying.

For surveys covering larger areas, however, the Earth's curvature must be considered. Such surveying is called geodetic; it must be very accurate, and geodetic instruments unusually precise.

See MAPPING AND SURVEYING in volume 23 of the Macropaedia.

Can an armadillo swim?

Armadilloes belong to the order of mammals known as Edentata, which also includes true anteaters and tree sloths. The entire history of the edentates is restricted to the Western hemisphere and most living species occur only in South America.

A persistent myth holds that all armadilloes can roll into an impregnable armour-plated ball as a defence against enemies. In fact, only the three-banded armadillo is able to perform this feat. Most can contort themselves into a reasonable facsimile of a ball, or flatten themselvs against the ground. Other means of escape, such as burrowing or feigning death, are common.

At a gallop some armadilloes can outpace a man. Because of their heavy armour, armadilloes have a specific gravity so high that they would normally sink in water. To overcome this problem, they gulp quanties of air to give them buoyancy for swimming. Alternatively, armadilloes seemingly take advantage of their specific gravity and cross small streams simply by walking under water on the bottom.

See MAMMALS in volume 23 of the Macropaedia.

What was the telharmonium?

During the 19th century, attempts were made to produce and record sounds mechanically or electromechanically. An important event was the invention of the phonograph in the 1870s and 1880s. An American, Thaddeus Cahill, later built a formidable assembly of rotary generators and telephone receivers to convert electrical signals into sound. Cahill called his invention the telharmonium. He started to build it in 1895 but it finally failed because it was complex and impractical. As amplifiers and loudspeakers had still to be invented, it could not produce sounds of any magnitude. Nevertheless, Cahill's concepts were basically sound and his instrument was the ancestor of present day electronic-music synthesizers.

Another ancestor of synthesized music was an Italian Futurist painter named Luigi Russolo. In 1913, proposing that all music be destroyed in favour of new instruments reflecting current technology, expressive of industrial society, he built a number of mechanically activated "noise instruments" that grated, hissed, scratched, rumbled, and shrieked. Russolo's instruments and most of his music apparently vanished during World War II.

See MUSICAL FORMS AND GENRES in volume 24 of the Macropaedia.

How is tea chosen for blending?

Teas bought at auction are blended and packaged by the traders to suit their own markets. Each firm bases its bidding on information provided by a tea taster, who notes the appearance of the dry tea, the infused leaf, and the infusion; the aroma of both the dry tea and the infused leaf; and the taste and flavour of the infusion.

The tea taster's infusion is made from a weight of tea equal to that of a silver sixpence (2·83 grams), which is infused in a China mug having a capacity of 0·12 litre and fitted with a lid. Boiling water is poured on the tea and allowed to stand for five or six minutes; the resulting liquor is poured into a handleless cup, and the infused leaf is shaken from the mug onto the lid. The liquor, without additives, is tasted at a temperature of about 43°C, usually from a spoon, after which it is spat out.

Teas to be used for a blend are selected for the quality, flavour, strength, and body of the liquors and the size, style, and density of the leaf. A proportion of neutral teas or "fillers" may be used to round off a blend and balance the price. The blend may include four or five Assam teas, the same number of Ceylons, and a few Africans. China teas usually blend well only with Darjeelings and fine Ceylons.

See Beverage Production in volume 14 of the Macropaedia.

What caused Ten Thousand Smokes?

In 1912 one of the most gigantic eruptions in history occurred in Alaska, after five days of violent earthquakes. Volcanic matter blasted into the atmosphere produced a high-altitude haze that robbed the northern temperate zone of an estimated 10 percent of the sun's heat during the summer of 1912.

The uninhabited site of the eruption was only located four years later, at which time the valley was alive with tens of thousands of jets of steam and gas ranging up to 649°C, issuing from vents, or fumaroles, in the earth up to 46 metres across. Over most of the valley, which was named Valley of Ten Thousand Smokes, ash lay to a depth of over 200 metres. All plant and animal life had been destroyed.

There are still mysteries associated with the cause and nature of the events that created the Valley of Ten Thousand Smokes. Plant life was slow to return and no animals live there, though moose and bear cross it from time to time.

See Valley of Ten Thousand Smokes in volume 11 of the Micropaedia.

Why do termites cultivate gardens?

Termites are cellulose-eating social insects that constitute the order Isoptera. There are about 1,900 species, which are most abundant in tropical rain forests. The termite colony is a highly organized unit, with division of labour among its members. Certain termites, known as the Macrotermitinae, cultivate symbiotic fungi in sponge-like "fungus gardens" or combs inside their nests. Fungi grow on the combs, and are eaten by the termites.

Termites are important to man in two ways. They are destructive when they feed upon, and often destroy, wooden structures or vegetable matter. However, they are also beneficial in that they help to convert plant cellulose into substances that can be recycled into the ecosystem to support new growth.

See Insects in volume 21 of the Macropaedia.

Who went rowing under *the Thames?*

Although designs for a craft to be navigated underwater were published in 1578 by William Bourne, a British mathematician and writer on naval subjects, Cornelis Drebbel, a Dutch inventor, is usually credited with building the first submarine. Between 1620 and 1624 he successfully manoeuvred his craft at depths of from four to five metres beneath the surface during repeated trials in the Thames. King James I is said to have gone aboard the craft for a short ride.

Drebbel's submarine resembled that proposed by Bourne in that its outer hull consisted of greased leather over a wooden frame; oars extended through the sides and, sealed with tight-fitting leather flaps, provided a means of propulsion both on the surface and underwater.

A number of submarine boats were conceived in the early years of the 18th century. By 1727 no fewer than 14 types had been patented in England alone. An unidentified inventor, whose work was described in the *Gentleman's Magazine* of 1747, proposed a submarine with goatskin bags attached to the hull with each skin connected to an aperture in the bottom of the craft. He planned to submerge the vessel by filling the skins with water and to surface by forcing the water out of the skins with a "twisting rod". This arrangement was a forerunner of the modern submarine ballast tank.

See Technology of War in volume 29 of the Macropaedia.

Why is the eruption of Thera famous?

About 1500 BC the volcano erupted on the island of Thera, 110 kilometres from Crete. The story of Atlantis, if Plato did not invent it, may reflect some Egyptian record of this eruption, one of the most stupendous of historical times. Knossos on Crete was shattered by a succession of earthquakes that preceded or accompanied the eruption, while great waves resulting from it appear to have damaged settlements along the northern coast of Crete. Later Greek traditions, such as the story of Deucalion's flood, may enshrine a memory of similar waves that swept the coast of the mainland at this time.

The settlements on Thera lay buried deep in pumice ash. The largest of these, at Akrotiri, opened by excavations since 1967, offers a unique picture of a Bronze Age town, the walls of the houses standing in places two stories high, with paintings miraculously preserved on them.

See GRECO-ROMAN CIVILIZATION in volume 20 of the Macropaedia.

How fast does a thunderstorm move?

The motion of a thunderstorm is determined largely by the average wind velocity in the layer of the atmosphere in which the storm develops. The average speed of 120 thunderstorms observed in Florida and Ohio was 20 kilometres per hour, but some storms moved much faster. In extreme circumstances thunderstorms may move at 80 kilometres per hour.

When considering the movement of a thunderstorm, the dynamic character of it must be taken into account. Most storms are in a constant state of change, with new cells developing while old ones dissipate. When wind speeds are light, an individual cell may move very little, less than 2 kilometres during its lifetime; but new cells forming downwind may give the illusion of rapid cloud motion. This type of behaviour is often observed in mountainous areas. The first storms of the day generally form over the ridges. As the day progresses, new clouds develop near the existing ones but closer to the valleys. An observer who sees the nearest edge of the clouds getting closer may readily assume that the original clouds are moving over the valley.

See CLIMATE AND WEATHER in volume 16 of the Macropaedia.

Does our body know what time it is?

The evolution of life on Earth has proceeded in the direction of maximal utilization of every habitable niche, with species specialized to deal with virtually every kind of environmental site. This specialization is related not only to space but also to time. The environment is in use full-time, but for maximal efficiency organisms work largely in "shifts". The night shift includes animals such as mice, cockroaches, moths, owls, and bats, the day shift includes songbirds, hawks, lizards, butterflies, and honeybees. Green plants alternate between daytime use of sunlight in photosynthesis and the night-time emphasis on growth and assimilation. Many plants undergo a daily sleep rhythm, their leaves drooping at night and rising by day.

In man, the daily alternation of sleep and wakefulness is accompanied by many changes. Daily variations occur in body temperature, in heart and respiratory rates, and in pressure and composition of the blood.

The variation in degree of resistance to physical and chemical insults over a 24-hour period is striking. Doses of X-rays that at one time of day can kill every individual exposed will at another time kill only a few individuals or none. Doses of powerful poisons, fully lethal at one time of day, leave animals unharmed at another. The effectiveness of alcohol, insulin, and even aspirin varies systematically with time of day.

Many organisms, man included, when removed from their natural surroundings and placed in the laboratory under constant conditions, can often repeat a rhythmic pattern that they had experienced before such isolation. Every living system studied behaves as if it contains a highly dependable clock.

See ANIMAL BEHAVIOUR in volume 14 of the Macropaedia.

Were totem poles meant for worship?

The tall totem poles of the Northwest Coast of America were not religious and were never intended to be worshipped. A totem pole recorded the social position, wealth, and relative importance of the person who had paid for it.

With the coming of the white man, who coveted the rich furs of the region, the Northwest Coast tribes acquired staggering wealth in an extremely brief space of time. The existence of an Indian purchasing class with its ever-increasing need for impressive possessions created a supplier, the professional artist.

More surprising, the works that were commissioned – including smaller wooden figures, masks, and other carved objects – were destined to be destroyed, given away, or neglected. For the life goal of many of these tribes was to give away their possessions. The logic was simple: the more one gave away, the greater one's prestige.

The rule was that the wealthy individual hold a feast to which his major rival was invited. The host would give away all his possessions, and the rival would return the courtesy, giving back more than he had received. To show even greater contempt for material possessions (and for one's rival) frequently goods were publicly burned, broken up, or cast into the sea. Slaves were even killed and families sold into slavery. From all this megalomania came the surviving aesthetic masterpieces that are valued so highly today.

See AMERICAN INDIANS in volume 13 of the Macropaedia.

What was a trebuchet?

Before the invention of gunpowder and the introduction of cannon into the armies of the world, the most effective long-range weapons for siege warfare were missile engines such as the catapult, the ballista (a kind of giant crossbow) and the trebuchet.

The trebuchet came into general use in the Middle Ages. It harnessed gravity by means of a weighted beam on a pivot. When the weighted end was raised and then released suddenly, a projectile loaded in a pocket at the other end of the beam could be thrown considerable distances.

All these ancient engines were used primarily for discharging projectiles, but they were also used to deliver flaming mixtures and even putrid animals or dead bodies (with the intention of causing disease).

See TECHNOLOGY OF WAR in volume 29 of the Macropaedia.

Why was trumpet king in New Orleans?

In New Orleans there was live music for births, weddings, christenings, funerals, picnics, parades, marches, and all kinds of celebrations. A great deal of this music was naturally played outdoors, which may explain the unchallenged dominance of the trumpet over all other instruments. All the early leaders of New Orleans jazz were trumpeters, with the line of succession passing down to Louis Armstrong.

In the classic New Orleans style, the trumpet's duty is to state and embellish the melodic line of the theme. The trombone stresses the harmonic root notes, providing also a solidity of resonance on which the other performers may build. Above the trumpet soars the clarinet voice, weaving further variations on the same harmonies. Thus the three voices, linked yet independent, are able to compile between them the simple triads (chords consisting of a root and the third and fifth tone above it) that were the basis of all jazz harmony at this period of its development. And, as all three were playing together throughout the performance, the band, though small, was able to maintain a surprising degree of volume.

See Musical Forms and Genres in volume 24 of the Macropaedia.

What lives on the tundra?

Fossil evidence indicates that in earlier geological ages many parts of the Arctic and Antarctic had temperate or warmer climates that led to quite luxuriant tree growth. Over millions of years the change to relative barrenness has occurred probably both through variations in world climate (the ice caps are no more than 4,500,000 years old) and from the drifting of landmasses poleward from lower latitudes.

Arctic and Antarctic plants and animals are extremely well adapted to their harsh and inhospitable environments. While terrestrial and freshwater life differs widely between the two regions, the far more prolific marine life is comparable, and it is chiefly in the seas that life abounds. In the Arctic vegetation is often fairly luxuriant in the southern tundra ranges, and the plants are very diverse, with more than 1,000 species of flowering plants and ferns known above the tree line; in marked contrast, the Antarctic proper possesses only three native flowering plants.

Arctic animals tend to be far less numerous than plants, both in species and individuals. The most notable among Arctic mammals on land are the Arctic hare, wolf, fox, lemming, polar bear, weasel, caribou, and musk-ox. The brown bear, red fox, and ermine range well into the Arctic without reaching as far north as these. As for the Antarctic, although several of the largest species of whale are found in its waters, it has no truly terrestrial vetebrates, and the largest terrestrial animals are two species of small midges.

See Ecosystems in volume 17 of the Macropaedia.

What is the future of the universe?

The remote future of the universe may be considered in the same spirit of speculation as its origins. In some 10^{10} years, the Sun will have evolved into a luminous red giant and have a radius much greater than at present, perhaps reaching the orbit of Mercury. The oceans will have disappeared and the Earth lost much of its present atmosphere, and life as it is now known will have become impossible if only because of the intense heat.

The gas and dust in the Galaxy must slowly disappear as it forms into new stars, and in 10^{10} years most stars will be old and only a very few will be young. Inevitably, in the course of time, the Milky Way will become faint and dark and the Galaxy a graveyard of stars that have reached the end point of stellar evolution, and similarly with other galaxies. Man, if he has survived, in a form beyond the wildest dreams of the 20th century, will have embarked on his last and perhaps greatest adventure.

According to steady-state theory, dying systems are forever superseded by new-born systems, and the general appearance of the universe will remain unchanged. But in the evolutionary cosmologies, the present dark and relatively empty universe is doomed to greater darkness and emptiness. If the Cosmos must forever expand, the glory of the early universe has departed forever, and an eternal future lies gripped in a frozen state of meaningless death.

See Cosmos in volume 16 of the Macropaedia.

Who was sneered at as an "upstart crow"?

William Shakespeare is widely regarded as the greatest writer of all time, but factual knowledge of his life is mostly gleaned from official documents with "flesh and blood" added to the

biograpical skeleton by a fair number of contemporary allusions to him as a writer.

After his marriage (where and when are not known exactly, but it was probably in 1582), and the birth of his children (Susanna in 1583, the twins Hamnet and Judith in 1584), Shakespeare evidently was based in London by the early 1590s.

How he spent the intervening years is unclear, but the first reference to him in the literary world comes in 1592. This was when a fellow dramatist, Robert Greene, declared in a pamphlet written on his deathbed (and clearly meant to be insulting to Shakespeare): "There is an upstart crow, beautified with our feathers, that with his *Tygers heart wrapt in a Players hide* supposes he is as well able to bombast out a blank verse as the best of you . . ." But the fact that after Greene's death a mutual acquaintance wrote a preface to the book offering an apology to Shakespeare and testifying to his worth indicates that the young playwright was already making important friends.

See the article on SHAKESPEARE in volume 27 of the Macropaedia.

Who were the first vegetarians?

Deliberate avoidance of flesh eating probably first appeared sporadically in ritual connections, either as a temporary purification or as qualification for a priestly function. Advocacy of a fleshless diet for normal use began around the middle of the 1st millennium BC in India and in eastern Mediterranean lands as part of the philosophical awakening of the time. In the Mediterranean, avoidance of flesh eating is first recorded as a teaching of Pythagoras. The Pythagoreans alleged the kinship of all animals as one basis for human benevolence towards other creatures, which should not be killed for food. From Plato onward many pagan philosophers recommended a fleshless diet; the idea carried with it condemnation of bloody sacrifices in worship and was often associated with belief in the reincarnation of souls.

With the transformation of Western and then world life in modern times, vegetarianism too entered a new phase. As part of the humanitarianism of the 17th and 18th centuries in Europe, with its confidence in moral progress, sensitiveness to animal suffering was revived and with it the Pythagorean disapproval of flesh eating. Vegetarians of the early 19th century appealed as much to the nutritional advantages of a light fare, in contrast with the rich and heavy meat diet of the day, as they did to ethical sensibilities.

See VEGETARIANISM in volume 12 of the Micropaedia.

What was "window" to the British, "chaff" to the Americans?

During World War II both sides recognized the importance of developing countermeasures to render enemy radars ineffectual. Jamming was a moderately successful, early technique of radar countermeasure that consisted of transmitting signals at the frequency of the enemy radar, so that his radar receiver was saturated or blocked and could not detect target signals.

One of the simplest, and yet most effective, methods of deluding radars consisted of dropping strips of aluminum foil from planes during raids to produce false echoes. Maximum return from the foil strips occurs when they are cut to a length of a half-wavelength. The Allies dropped long strips cut to a half-wavelength at the low frequency of the German radars while the Germans dropped short strips to yield false echoes for the micro-wave radars used by the Allies.

On a full-scale bombing raid, the Royal Air Force dispensed enough foil to equal the weight of three bombers. The foil was called window by the British, chaff by the Americans and *Dueppel* by the Germans.

See MEASUREMENT AND OBSERVATION in volume 23 of the Macropaedia.

What is a portmanteau word?

Words are sometimes blended, by being telescoped. An example is "motorcade" from "motorcavalcade". A travel monologue becomes a travelogue, and a telegram sent by cable a cablegram. Biology electronics becomes bionics, and a pulsating star becomes a pulsar.

English, widely spoken on all six continents, also has a strong effect on many regions where it is not the principal language. The portmanteau words Franglais and Japlish, for example, have been invented by resentful purists to describe the numerous expressions resulting from the infiltration of English into French and Japanese. The vocabulary of modern English is approximately half Germanic (Old English and Scandinavian) and half Italic or Romance (French and Latin), with importations from Greek, Dutch, Low German, Italian, Spanish, German, Arabic, and many other languages.

See LANGUAGES OF THE WORLD in volume 22 of the Macropaedia.

Does a surgeon always close the wound after operating?

In surgery, there are two general techniques of wound treatment; the closed technique, in which all tissues, including the skin, are closed with suture material after completion of the operation; and the open technique, in which the wound is left open, to be closed later. The open technique is used in badly contaminated wounds in which infection might be anticipated if immediate closure were done. Open treatment allows wound drainage and thus avoids entrapment of micro-organisms, while also permitting observation of the wound.

See DIAGNOSIS AND THERAPEUTICS in volume 17 of the Macropaedia.

Could Zeppelins have bombed New York?

At the start of World War I the German Navy had one Zeppelin airship and the Army six, plus three converted commercial Zeppelins and three smaller airships. The army made the mistake of sending its Zeppelins over heavily defended areas in daylight, and three were shot down before the end of the first month of the war.

Thereafter the German Navy achieved outstanding successes in the North Sea with Zeppelins, keeping constant watch on Allied shipping movements. Naval airships also spearheaded German air attacks on Britain. In 51 raids between Jan. 19, 1915 and Aug. 5, 1918 they dropped 5,806 bombs.

Finest of the Zeppelins was LZ-70, commanded by Fregattenkapitän Peter Strasser. The LZ-70 was 225 metres long and able to fly above 4,900 metres. It had a range of over 12,000 kilometres, which enabled Strasser to plan an air raid on New York by three such craft. Before this could be attempted, the LZ-70 was shot down.

See TECHNOLOGY OF WAR in volume 29 of the Macropaedia.

How long have there been zoos?

The word zoo was first used about 100 years ago as a popular abbreviation for the zoological gardens in London. Zoos, as places where wild animals are exhibited in captivity, are much older, and it is possible they were associated with the first attempts at animal domestication.

Tame antelopes are depicted in Egyptian tombs from about 2500 BC, while in China Wen Wang (*c.*1000 BC) built a large zoo which he named the Garden of Intelligence. King Solomon was another contemporary zoo-keeper, and animal collections were a feature of many royal establishments. Most were kept as public spectacles, but the Greeks of Aristotle's time were more concerned with study and experiment. Aristotle's most famous pupil, Alexander the Great, sent back to Greece many animals caught on his military expeditions.

Zoos declined with the end of the Roman Empire, but animal collections were maintained by the Emperor Charlemagne in the 8th century AD and by Henry I in the 12th century. In the New World, Hernan Cortes discovered a magnificent zoo in Mexico in 1519. Modern zoo keeping however, dates from 1752 and the founding of the Imperial Menagerie in Vienna. Other zoos opened in Madrid and Paris in the 18th century and the Zoological Society of London established its collection in Regent's Park in 1828, two years after the Society itself was founded.

See ZOO in volume 12 of the Micropaedia.